PROFESSOR CALCULUS:
Science's Forgotten Genius

With special thanks to Tim Jones

First published in French in 1994 by Casterman
This edition first published in Great Britain 2023 by Farshore
An imprint of HarperCollins*Publishers*
1 London Bridge Street, London SE1 9GF
www.farshore.co.uk

HarperCollins*Publishers*
Macken House, 39/40 Mayor Street Upper,
Dublin 1, D01 C9W8, Ireland

Image Creditst:
Page 32 © Everett Collection Historical / Alamy
Page 35 © Associated Press / Alamy
Page 36 and 37 La Plongée Du Pélican © Éditions Du Triomphe
Page 41 © US Air Force Medical Service
Page 44 © Roger Violett
Page 54 L'Astronautique © Alexandre Ananoff

ISBN 978 0 00 861516 1
Printed in Estonia by Printbest
001

A CIP catalogue record for this title is available from the British Library.

This book is produced from independently certified FSC™ paper
to ensure responsible forest management.

For more information visit: www.harpercollins.co.uk/green

ALBERT ALGOUD

PROFESSOR CALCULUS:
Science's Forgotten Genius

One day, when I was young, my
mum and dad gave me a copy of
Red Rackham's Treasure.
I can never thank them enough
for this wonderful gift, which
introduced me to Professor Calculus.
I therefore dedicate this book to them.

A.A

CONTENTS

A TRIBUTE TO A FORGOTTEN MAN IN THE HISTORY OF SCIENCE

To capture the collective imagination, a fictional scientist has to be wholly mad[1], like Fritz Lang's Dr Mabuse, or politely deranged, in the style of Hergé's Calculus. One thing that's for certain is that the Professor, inventor of the first moon rocket and the clothes brushing machine, has long embodied the trope of the absent-minded scientist. A literary noble tradition following in the footsteps of Jules Verne with Aristobulus Ursiclos[2] and Zéphirin Xirdal[3], Christophe with Cosinus[4] or André Daix with Professor Nimbus[5]. But compared with his eminent colleagues, what is it that makes our subject so unique?

It is simply that as soon as you say the name Professor Calculus, it conjures up an old-fashioned image of a frail diminutive man bobbing around in a green raincoat, wearing an old hat and carrying an umbrella. The goatee, the moustache and his remnant of thick hair, like a fragment of one of Saturn's rings, otherworldly hair for an otherworldly mind. He is instantly recognisable. The great originality of Calculus is that he is extraordinarily familiar to us.

Yet, paradoxically, although Calculus is so famous, it is clear that his unique genius remains unrecognised!

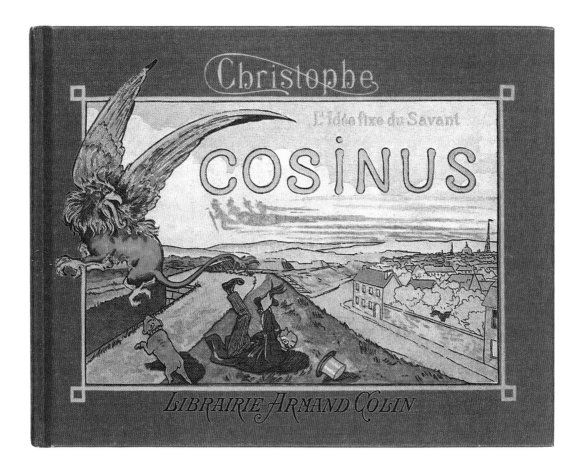

Christophe

L'Idée fixe du Savant

COSINUS

LIBRAIRIE ARMAND COLIN

The singular temperament of Hergé's character alone is not enough to hold the attention of posterity. A brilliant scientist, the Learned Calculus, remains implausibly absent from dictionaries and encyclopaedias. Worse still, the History of Science blissfully ignores him[6].

So much so, that at the time of writing these indignant lines, no epistemologist[7] has deigned to cite the theories and discoveries of Calculus, even though they are of paramount importance. While Robert H. Goddard (1882-1945) and Serge Korolev (1906-1966) are presented as the two pioneers of space exploration, we forget that it is because of Calculus that man has fulfilled one of his oldest dreams: walking on the moon! This scandal has gone on for far too long, and it is in order to deservedly celebrate this scientist – who knew how to exalt technical power and the mastery of nature without seeking domination that this book has been written.

The scientist, Cosinus

1. Omnibus has published a fascinating anthology dedicated to mad scientists. Paris 1994.
2. The Green Ray (1882).
3. Chase of the Golden Meteor (1908).
4. L'idée fixe du savant Cosinus (1899).
5. The Professor Nimbus (1934).
6. Le livre mondial des inventions, Fixot 1993, does not mention Calculus once!
7. The foundation in July 1991 of the Cuthbert Calculus Faculty of Tintinology is an exception to this conspiracy of silence, the academic body of this Faculty having, among other things, assigned itself the task of deepening and teaching all the disciplines mastered by Calculus.

Sunflower (Calculus's name in the French original, tournesol), from the Italian tornasole. This annual plant of great height evokes the sun through its inflorescence and beautiful yellow colouring, making it worthy of its popular name.

Being heliotropic, it turns towards the sun, which is where its name Helianthus comes from (from the Greek helios, meaning sun, and anthos, meaning flower).

Sunflowers. Van Gogh. Arles 1889. Vincent Van Gogh Stichting. Van Gogh Museum, Amsterdam.

"Calculus came to me, I don't know how..."[8] If Hergé is to be believed, the professor's name cannot be explained. However, if we refer to the theory of the psychoanalyst Jacques Lacan, according to which we always bear the name we deserve, wouldn't this idea of nominative determinism explain the Professor's strange name?

AN APPROPRIATE NAME: CALCULUS

A MAN OF SCIENCE

Calculus is the mathematical discipline of continuous change. It derives from the Latin word for 'small pebble' from the Latin calx, meaning 'stone'. In the Roman era these small pebbles were used for counting, somewhat similar to an abacus. Calculus is the result of the work of the two mathematical giants of Newton and Leibniz. The name evokes both the complexity and eccentricity of the Professor's character.

As something of a polymath, it is to be expected that the Professor has an in-depth knowledge of calculus, both differential and integral. The name also contains a suggestion of the calculations so vital to the Professor's scientific success. His achievements in every part of science, from engineering to astrophysics, attest to the appropriateness of his peculiar moniker.

In *Red Rackham's Treasure*, Calculus deciphers the documents found in the wreck of *The Unicorn*, thereby unlocking the secret of the story. With the huge sum paid for the patent of his shark submarine, he can afford to buy Captain Haddock's ancestral home, Marlinspike Hall, thereby generously restoring it to the Haddock family. If there is a conundrum to be solved, Calculus will find a way.

Illustrious Forebears

We owe the invention of Calculus to Isaac Newton (1642-1746) and Gottfried Wilhelm Leibniz (1646-1714), who invented the new mathematical study contemporaneously. Initially Newton accused Leibniz of plagiarism, something that the professor himself would later encounter during his invention of the moon rocket, which bore some similarities to the V2 of Werner Von Braun. Eventually however, Leibniz and Newton were given joint credit for the discovery, though Leibniz was responsible for developing much of the notation. This was partly because Newton used an idiosyncratic method to record his findings. Given Professor Calculus's carelessness with keeping hold of the records of his work, as shown in the events of *The Calculus Affair*, it seems that the professor himself is more of a Newtonian than a Leibnizian. It cannot be doubted, however, that he must have had a great deal of respect for the work of both the originators of calculus, and stood on their shoulders as he added to the extent of human scientific advancement with his own inventions.

Gotfried Von Leibniz

Isaac Newton

8. Numa Sadoul, Entretiens avec Hergé, Casterman 1975.

Like that of Captain Haddock, the professor's name lends itself to entertaining distortions.

In *The Calculus Affair*, he is called Candyfloss (p. 39, 10) then Coelacanth (p. 39, 12) by the man who Tintin and Haddock suspect of having kidnapped him. Castafiore in turn calls him Candyfloss (*The Castafiore Emerald*, p. 43, 3). And Jolyon Wagg, exclaims: "Same old Calculoopy!" (*Flight 714 to Sydney*, p. 61, 5.)

There! Now where's your Coelacanth? Inside the spare wheel, I suppose.

The incorrupt body of Saint Cuthbert (from Bede's Life of Cuthbert, 12th Century).

The professor's Christian name, in keeping with the eccentric surname it is paired with, is redolent of learning and wisdom. The alliterative pairing denotes Calculus's strength of character and fortitude in the face of travail, much like his namesake St. Cuthbert. Amongst the many famous Cuthberts that succeed the saint, we find a winner of the Victoria Cross, a zoologist famous for his work on sleeping sickness, and a Royal Navy Vice-Admiral who was a key figure in the battle of Trafalgar – to which prestigious list we can now add our very own professor.

A SACRED CHRISTIAN NAME: CUTHBERT

A MIRACULOUS LIFE?

The name of Cuthbert has been bestowed on many a luminary, but the best known is perhaps the saint of that name.

Born in Dunbar, UK, in the mid-630s, he was a missionary, priest and bishop, dedicating himself to an ascetic monastic life in dedication to his chosen field in much the same way as Calculus. He was credited with a number of miracles, and according to Bede's

text *Life of Cuthbert*, when Cuthbert's sarcophagus was opened eleven years after his death, his body was found to be completely preserved and untouched by decomposition.

During the saint's lifetime, the English church progressed from following the Celtic tradition to the Roman one, and Calculus himself goes through something of a conversion on meeting Tintin and Captain Haddock – certainly his life is never quite the same again.

Cuthberts Brave and True
Our very own professor certainly has the heart of a lion, as we find whenever his hackles rise. As a Cuthbert he is not alone in this attribute – take for example Lord Collingwood, Nelson's second-in-command at the Battle of Trafalgar in 1804. As the captain of the second column of the British fleet, Cuthbert Collingwood showed immense bravery in tackling the Franco-Spanish fleet. Although outnumbered, the British ships won the day, though at

the cost of Lord Nelson's life. It was Cuthbert Collingwood who, following the Admiral's demise, took command of the victorious British fleet and sailed home a hero.

Another illustrious Cuthbert was Major Cuthbert Bromley, awarded the highest award for valour in the British Army, The Victoria Cross. He won this seldom-awarded medal during a landing at Gallipoli in April 1915, but as with many other VC winners, did not survive the conflict he fought in – he was killed when his ship was sunk by a U-Boat in the Mediterranean.

Some specialists thought they had identified this as the young Cuthbert Calculus indulging in the joys of ice skating. However, this could not be confirmed.

What was life like for Cuthbert Calculus before his pivotal encounter with Tintin and Captain Haddock? If we cannot piece together this huge missing section of his biography, certain clues allow us to at least see things a little more clearly.

CUTHBERT CALCULUS BEFORE TINTIN

EARLY LIFE AND SPORTS

An Olympic athlete

In *Red Rackham's Treasure* (p. 35), while rowing energetically in search of Tintin, Calculus confides in Haddock that he owes the preservation of his svelt figure to athletics, and especially to walking. A confession that, a short time later (*Red Rackham's Treasure*, p. 52), earns him treatment as a kind of "Olympic athlete" by the Captain. Furthermore, in *Flight 714 to Sydney* (p. 7), the professor reveals that he not only did horse riding, but also took part in tennis, swimming, football, rugby, fencing, skating, wrestling, boxing and savate.

Tennis, swimming, rugger, soccer, fencing, skating . . . I did them all in my young days. Not forgetting the ring, too: wrestling, boxing, and even savate . . .

Savate? . . .

Savate

As French boxing or savate was very fashionable at the end of the 19th century and during the *Belle Époque* era in the mid-1800s, in referring to the practice of this sport, Calculus shows himself to be a man of a certain age who owes having stayed young and having retained the agility of his twenties to this athletic activity.

Here too, the resemblance of the boxer on the right, with Cuthbert, as remarkable as it is, could not be verified.

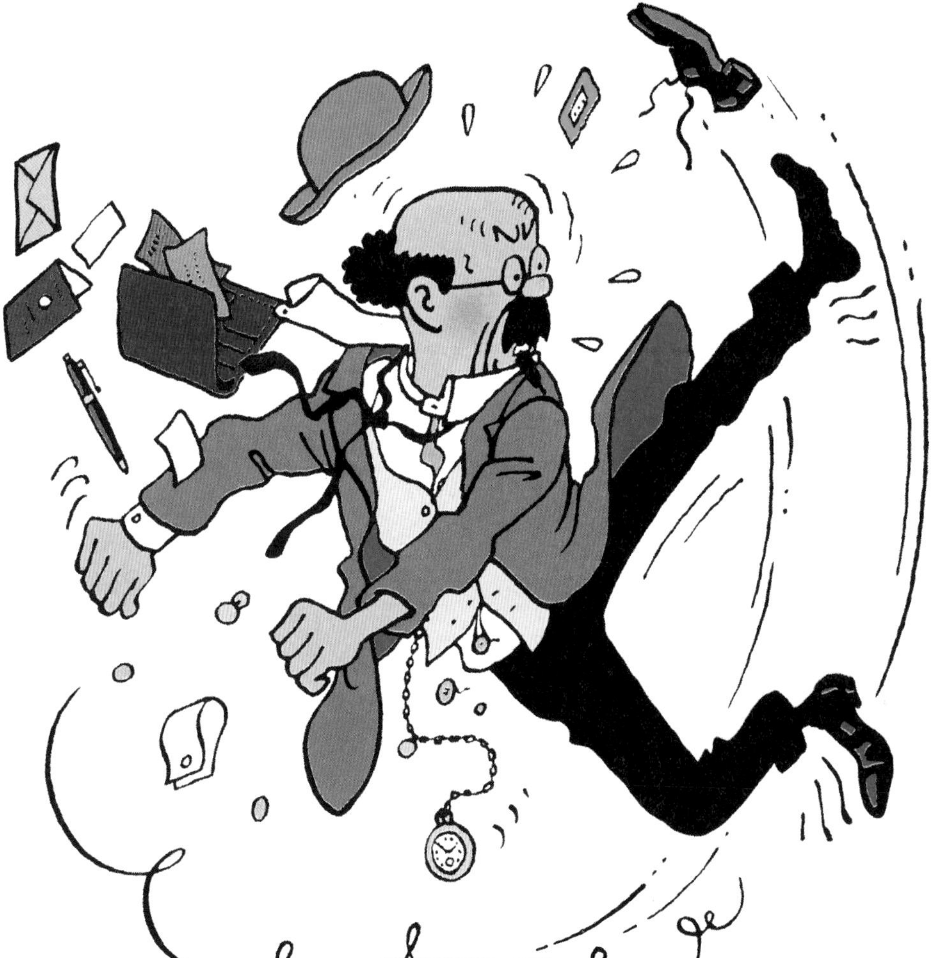

Studies

In *The Seven Crystal Balls*, we learn that Cuthbert studied with Hercules Tarragon (*The Seven Crystal Balls*, p. 26). Since Tarragon has become an Americanist, while Calculus turned towards primarily scientific disciplines, we can conclude that the studies in question must be their secondary education, perhaps even their primary education too. This makes Cuthbert and Hercules childhood friends who have known each other for a long time, as is suggested by Tarragon's affectionate exclamation as he lifts his friend into his arms: "Well, well; dear old Cuthbert!" (*The Seven Crystal Balls*, p. 27).

Family

We know absolutely nothing about the professor's parents. The only hint he gives us about his family is not helpful, as he tells Tintin that he never had a sister! (*Tintin and the Picaros*, p. 42).

Career

It is the same story for Calculus' career before he met Tintin as with our knowledge of his family: here, once again, we know nothing. Nothing, other than the Professor was previously not very highly regarded and seemed to live frugally.

In a top-floor flat, perhaps even a converted attic, Calculus experiments with hypothetically useful inventions that more reflect the work of an amateur enthusiast rather than that of a scientist of international renown, to whom man owes having walked on the Moon.

Even if the possibility is shocking, it must be considered with bravery and without outcry; you can bet that had he not met Tintin, Calculus would have remained, what we can only refer to as a failure. Furthermore, if the title of professor implies that he had to teach, the dreadful bedlam that would have disturbed his classes is unimaginable.

Gentlemen, I'd like to read you a signal we've just picked up. It's a distress call. The text is disjointed, as if the transmitter was damaged. Even the name of the ship is incomplete.

Even if Calculus's family background remains unclear, we can, however, retrace the origins of this character by examining the professors who intermittently appeared before him.

THE PROFESSORS BEFORE CALCULUS

The anonymous professor from *The Broken Ear*
An unidentified professor appeared at the beginning of *The Broken Ear*. His complete absent-mindedness is reminiscent of that of Calculus (*The Broken Ear* p. 6).

Sophocles Sarcophagus
Tintin first becomes acquainted with this Egyptologist, who has left for Egypt with the aim of unearthing the tomb of

Pharoah Kih-Oskh, on board the M.S. Isis, a cruise liner taking him towards the Far East. It should be noted that Tintin always bonds with the scientists who play an important part in his life on board a ship, the scientist having embarked on a search for a valuable artifact: Professor Phostle on board the Aurora in his quest to find the meteorite, and Professor Calculus on board the Sirius trying to recover the lost treasure of

Red Rackham. He also meets Captain Haddock in the hold of the Karaboudjan.

Absent-mindedness is Sophocles Sarcophagus's main personality trait and primarily relates to the identification of those around him. Taking his leave of Snowy (*Cigars of the Pharoah*, p. 3), he says "Goodbye, young man." Upon finding Tintin in Port Said, he greets him with "Happy New Year!" (*Cigars of the Pharoah*, p. 5). This absent-mindedness, however, verges on impaired thinking and it is not surprising that Sophocles Sarcophagus has sunk into madness when Tintin finds him roaming the jungle (*Cigars of the Pharoah*, p. 36 to 43).

All evidence could lead us to believe that this singular Egyptologist had been the victim of Rajaijah juice, the poison that makes you go insane. Nevertheless, it could be imagined that it was partially the swirling mental cyclone in his mind that had finally overcome his sanity. Having become insane, Sarcophagus continues to confuse people's identities, behaviour that was previously chalked up to his significant absent-mindedness. When he

leaves the hospital where Tintin has just been wrongfully detained in his place, he calls back to the director of the institution, a solidly built, bearded man in a white coat, "Happy birthday, Nanny!" (*Cigars of the Pharoah*, p. 44).

To all intents and purposes insane, Sarcophagus was close to being consumed completely by the schizophrenia that was subverting his own identity.

Literally possessed by his scientific discipline, the Egyptologist ends up convinced that he is Pharoah Rameses II.

Fang Hsi-Ying

Professor Fang Hsi-Ying is as wise as Professor Sarcophagus is mad. As if to restore stability, a reassuring scientist appeared in *The Blue Lotus*, which was originally the sequel to *Cigars of the Pharoah*.

Sophocles Sarcophagus was committed to the mental hospital in Gaipajama for several years, but was released in 1955, when he was eventually deemed to no longer be dangerous by the psychiatrists treating him.

Refusing to return to Europe, he was assigned to caring for the sacred elephants at the behest of the Maharajah of Gopal.

The last witnesses to have seen him stated that he had henceforth taken to calling himself Ganesh, the name of the elephant-headed god who is the patron of intellectual pursuits.

Fang Hsi-Ying, a psychiatrist of international renown, who Tintin finds out about while watching a newsreel in a cinema in Shanghai, is made famous because he is the "world authority on madness" (*The Blue Lotus*, p. 33).

The anti-Sarcophagus

Fang Hsi-Ying is therefore the anti-Sarcophagus, who hunts for breakdowns, and it is he who discovers the antidote for Rajaijah juice, also saving Didi, Wang's son, from madness. Kidnapped as a result of his expertise and rescued by Tintin, he would understand more than most the plight Calculus suffers on two future occasions.

When the *Seven Crystal Balls* appeared, the upheaval of the Second World War prevented the psychiatrists trying to treat the victims of Rascar Capac's revenge from contacting their fellow psychiatrist Fang Hsi-Ying and asking his advice. During the Cultural Revolution, Fang Hsi-Ying refused orders by the Red Guard to publicly criticise his own work and was sentenced to hard labour in the Gobi Desert.

Investigations undertaken by this author with the goal of finding Fang Hsi-Ying were not as successful as those of Hergé, which allowed his friend Chang to return to Europe.

Albert Algoud

Paris, 22 August 1993

Dear Ambassador,

In Brussels in 1981, after a lengthy period of separation, the cartoonist Hergé tracked down his friend and your fellow countryman, the sculptor Chang Chong-jen, of whom he had heard no news for a very long time.

This reunion restored my hope of finding the whereabouts of another of your fellow countrymen, Professor Fang Hsi-Ying, a specialist in mental illness. Regrettably, my enquiries in Shanghai, where he lived, have remained futile and unanswered.

It is for this reason, Ambassador, that I turn to you for help in my endeavours. I would be very grateful if you would kindly direct me as to which authorities of the People's Republic of China I could address myself to, in order to trace Professor Fang Hsi-Ying.

I express my sincere appreciation in advance for any thought you give to my request, and please allow me to express my deepest respect for you.

Albert Algoud

Hector Alembick

Scholar of sigillography. "Sigillography is the science concerned with the study of seals." (*King Ottokar's Sceptre*, p. 2) Hector Alembick is a forgetful man. It is because he left his suitcase on a park bench that Tintin, who returns it, meets him and agrees to accompany him to Syldavia.

A convoluted plan à la Alembick

These travel plans are frustrated by the activities of Syldavian revolutionaries.

In order to gain possession of Ottokar's sceptre and to bring down the monarchy, these revolutionaries hatched a plan that was convoluted to say the least: kidnap Hector Alembick and replace him with his twin brother Alfred, their accomplice!

Whereas Hector is blind and smokes like a chimney, Tintin later finds it strange that he can identify barely-visible sheep with the naked eye and doesn't smoke a single cigarette.

Nowadays, Hector Alembick is continuing his work, at the head of the International Federation of Sigillography.

After several years' incarceration in Kragoniedin Prison, Alfred Alembick was pardoned by King Muskar XII. Having reverted to being an arms trader, he is rumoured to have been involved in several conflicts in the Balkan region, suggesting that he not so much mended his ways but found a new expression for them.

Decimus Phostle, the definitive forerunner to Calculus

Director of the Observatory and the key protagonist of *The Shooting Star*, this astronomer is the scientist who most strongly foreshadows Calculus, who makes his appearance shortly afterwards in *Red Rackham's Treasure*. Although the craniums of the two scientists vary considerably in terms of shape and size – Phostle's head is as elongated as Calculus's is flat – what occupies the minds of these two "brains" uniquely connects them.

They both discover a metal previously unknown on Earth: Phostle discovers *phostlite* and Calculus, *cobalt in the natural state* (*Flight 714 to Sydney*, p. 61). Both professors also show a distinct interest in very complicated calculations. Interestingly, both scientists miss out on their final calculation being related to a cosmic collision.

In this way, Professor Phostle identifies the precise time (12 minutes and 30 seconds past 8) at which a gigantic meteorite is going to collide with the earth (*The Shooting Star*, p. 6). On his way to the moon, Calculus devises an automated system controlled by radar that steers the rocket's controls to prevent the rocket from having "a collision with the meteorite" (*Explorers on the Moon*, p. 14). Like Calculus, Phostle can suddenly switch from being extremely rational to being completely irrational. After having exclaimed: "I, Decimus Phostle, have determined the moment at which the cataclysm will befall us," he adds, disregarding all logic regarding the imminent chain of events, "tomorrow I shall be famous!" (*The Shooting Star*, p. 6).

Rather than celebrate having escaped nothing less than the end of the world and therefore certain offence when Tintin dares to suggest that it could have been him who made a mistake in his calculations. "You'd dare to deceive us?" But, just as Calculus does on board *Sirius*, Phostle becomes more understanding during an expedition at sea.

Leading this important mission, which gives responsibilities to this individual who had previously shown himself to be so bizarrely egotistical, means he comes to feel solidarity with the men who he shares the hardships of daily life with.

His paternal attentiveness is mainly directed towards the young Tintin: "You ought to put on warm clothes: you'll catch cold going about like that," "I should have told him to be careful on the deck" (*The Shooting Star*, p. 27).

9. "The quest for the Holy Grail always symbolises spiritual adventure and demands on the inner self. Tintin learnt this reading Jung and, during his travels, realises that the treasures that we travel far and wide in search of can be found in the here and now." Remy Cornerotte, L'univers d'Hergé, The Hergé Foundation.

It is not unreasonable to see a real transformation in this evolution of character, as, little by little, Phostle allows his better self to emerge during this quest, which – as is often the case in the adventures of Tintin – doubles as an opportunity for self-reflection and discovery.[9] In the face of danger, Phostle speaks from the heart: "Let's hope they don't run into any trouble" (*The Shooting Star*, p. 33). The emotions of a worried heart prevail over the cold calculations of an unfeeling head. And when, after having received an apparent S.O.S., Haddock solemnly asks the professor whether they ought to divert their journey to rescue the ship in distress, or continue with their mission, Phostle does

not hesitate for a second: "We must go to their aid, even if it does cost us our prize" (*The Shooting Star*, p. 38).

By making this extreme sacrifice, the professor abandons the vanity of pursuing worldly honours and even forgets his original mission in favour of the more noble one of saving souls in distress. The letters S.O.S. are, after all, the initials for the phrase 'save our souls.'

In this burst of redeeming compassion, Phostle, whose name is then haloed in a symbolic light, reaches a Christ-like glory.

Philippulus the Prophet

A former colleague of Professor Phostle, who, on further inspection, he closely resembles, Philippulus believes himself to be a prophet and proclaims the imminent approach of the end of the world (*The Shooting Star*, p. 7, 12).

Phostle's scientific predictions for that nightmarish night preceding the apocalypse do not conflict with Philippulus's dramatic prophecies, as if the rational and the irrational had coincided. Once more, we see that the danger that awaits scientists is that of being obsessed with their own knowledge to the point of ceasing to understand it.

Furthermore, the schizophrenia accompanied by fits of violence that affects Philippulus very much echoes that of Sophocles Sarcophagus. As a penitent scientist, Philippulus is the only scientist in the adventures of Tintin to make such a strong reference to the divine.

In his eyes, science is a sinful enterprise, and anyone who associates with it, like Tintin, is "an advocate of the devil, a son of Satan, a tool of Beelzebub!" (*The Shooting Star*, p. 8), and deserves punishing for having dared to usurp the divine powers.

Re-committed to the mental hospital that he had escaped from, Philippulus broke out once again in 1950.

Having clandestinely travelled to the United States, he founded the cult of the "Arachnidians of the Apocalypse". Having proclaimed himself Dean of the university opened entirely lawfully in the state of Texas, he held the position of chair of "prophetic epidemiology" until 1968, the year when he passed away, stung by a European garden spider, a giant species of spider whose cult he had established.

Scientists of the E.F.S.R. expedition:

Björgenskjöld (*Erik*)
This Swedish astronomer is the author of "distinguished papers on solar prominences". His specialism and his international renown account for his participation in the expedition in search of the shooting star.

Bolero y Calamares (*Porfirio*)
A professor at the University of Salamanca in Spain, he also participates in the expedition financed by the European Fund for Scientific Research, however his specialism remains unspecified.

Cantonneau (*Paul*)
This Swiss scholar from the University of Freiburg also takes part in the expedition initiated to find the meteorite from the shooting star.

In *The Seven Crystal Balls* (p. 20, 7-11), we meet him in Brussels, where he, in turn, falls victim to the curse of Rascar Capac.

At the end of *Prisoners of the Sun* (p. 60), when the curse is lifted and the image in his likeness is thrown into the fire, he comes out of his long slumber.

Dos Santos *(Pedro Joãs)*
A renowned physicist, of the University of Coimbra, he also embarks on the Aurora.

Schulze *(Herr Doktor Otto)*
Professor at the University of Munich, we do not know his specialism.

Auguste Piccard in 1931 waves as he climbs into the spherical aluminum capsule. In this first attempt to ascend to the stratosphere, the balloon did not provide sufficient lift.

"Physically, Calculus and his submarine were also based on Professor Auguste Piccard and his bathyscaphe, but a shorter version of Piccard, because the genuine one was very tall. He had an extremely long neck that emerged from a too-large collar. I sometimes ran into him in the street[10] and he seemed to me to be the very epitome of the "scholar." I designed Calculus as a miniature Piccard, otherwise I would have had to enlarge the sketch panels!"[11]

PROFESSOR AUGUSTE PICCARD (1884-1962)

In 1931, the Swiss Inventor and Professor August Piccard became the first man to explore the stratosphere, travelling beyond an altitude of 18,000 metres in his hot-air balloon, the FNRS 1. It was during one of his ascents that he found the solution for his bathyscaphe (a deep-sea diving vehicle) project.

FNRS 2
His bathyscaphe was designed similarly to his airship, which consisted of a basket suspended from a balloon filled with a gas lighter than air. His bathyscaphe is a 9cm-thick steel sphere with an internal diameter of 2m, suspended in a tank that functions as a floatation device, which is filled with a gas lighter than water and which equalises pressure with the external environment by means of a system of valves. Besides seven tanks of gas, the flotation device contains some cannisters of iron and lead shot, for descending and ascending. In 1948, a first, unladen attempt managed to reach a depth of 1000m. Unfortunately, even before having dived with passengers, the FNRS 2 could not withstand surface waves. Battering against the hull of the support ship, the flotation device was quickly smashed apart.

FNRS 3
However, Auguste Piccard was not discouraged. He built a new bathyscaphe, fitted with the sphere from FNRS 2 but combined with a much more robust flotation device. In February 1954, it managed a dive to 4050m.

Not feeling adequately supported by the French state, Auguste Piccard developed a new bathyscape, the Trieste, with the help of Swiss and Italian funds, which carried out a dive to 3150m in 1953. The performance of the Trieste having caught the attention of the United States, the US Navy built the Trieste 2, which reached the depth of 10,916m on 23 January 1960, with Jacques Piccard (Auguste's son) and the first lieutenant Don Walsh on board: a record that will never be beaten.

If Auguste Piccard shows some physical resemblance to Cuthbert Calculus, except his height – bald head, moustache, small round glasses[12]– we nevertheless notice that the career of the former started in the stratosphere and continued under the sea, whereas that of the latter follows the exact opposite trajectory. If we refer to the first publication of *Red Rackham's Treasure* (1943), we also notice that Calculus' revolutionary submarine was conceived and developed long before Auguste Piccard's first bathyscaphe, FNRS 2, which was built in 1948. From here, we must go only one step further, to conclude that it was Calculus who inspired Piccard, and not the other way around.

It should also be noted that Auguste Piccard had a twin brother, Jean, who was a stratonaut like him.

Lastly, Bianca Castafiore, the renowned opera singer refers to Professor Piccard when, mistaking Calculus's identity when Tintin introduces him for the first time, she exclaims "How enchanting, how absolutely thrilling to meet you; the man who makes all those daring ascents in balloons!" (*The Castafiore Emerald*, p. 9).

10. Of Swiss nationality, Professor Piccard taught in Brussels.
11. Numa Sadoul, Entretiens avec Hergé, Casterman 1975, p. 106.
12. In The Shooting Star, Auguste Piccard is part of the delegation from the European Funds for Scientific Research that comes to return the flag that is later planted on top of the meteorite to Professor Calculus. Page 21, panel 2, he is the first on the right.

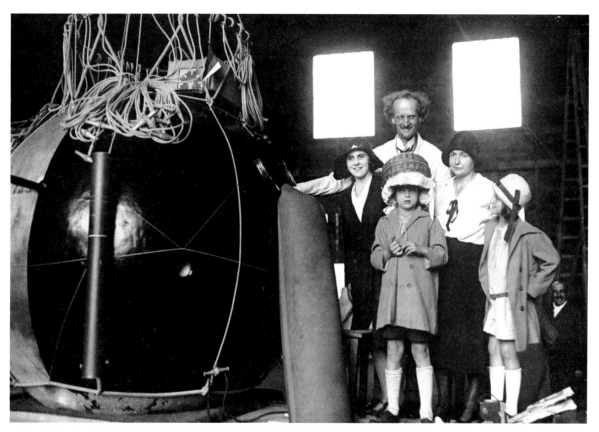

Professor Auguste Piccard with his wife and family photographed beside the metal
cylinder in which he successfully made the ascent 10 miles from Augsberg on May, 1931.

Between 4th July 1954 and 29th May 1955, *La plongée du Pélican*[13] appeared in the French comic series "Fripounet et Marisette." One of the protagonists of the exciting story, Professor Luke Nebulus, inventor of a bathyscaphe, inevitably makes us think of Auguste Piccard and of Professor Calculus. Because he is very similar to the former, he is afflicted by the great absent-mindedness of the latter.

13. Text and drawings by the talented René Bonnet, all of whose books were originally published by Fleurus Editions and were republished by the Fleurus Archives, then by Éditions du Triomphe.

LES AVENTURES DE
FRIPOUNET ET MARISETTE

SCÉNARIO ET
ILLUSTRATIONS DE
R. Bonnet

LA PLONGÉE
DU
"PÉLICAN"

EDITIONS DU TRIOMPHE

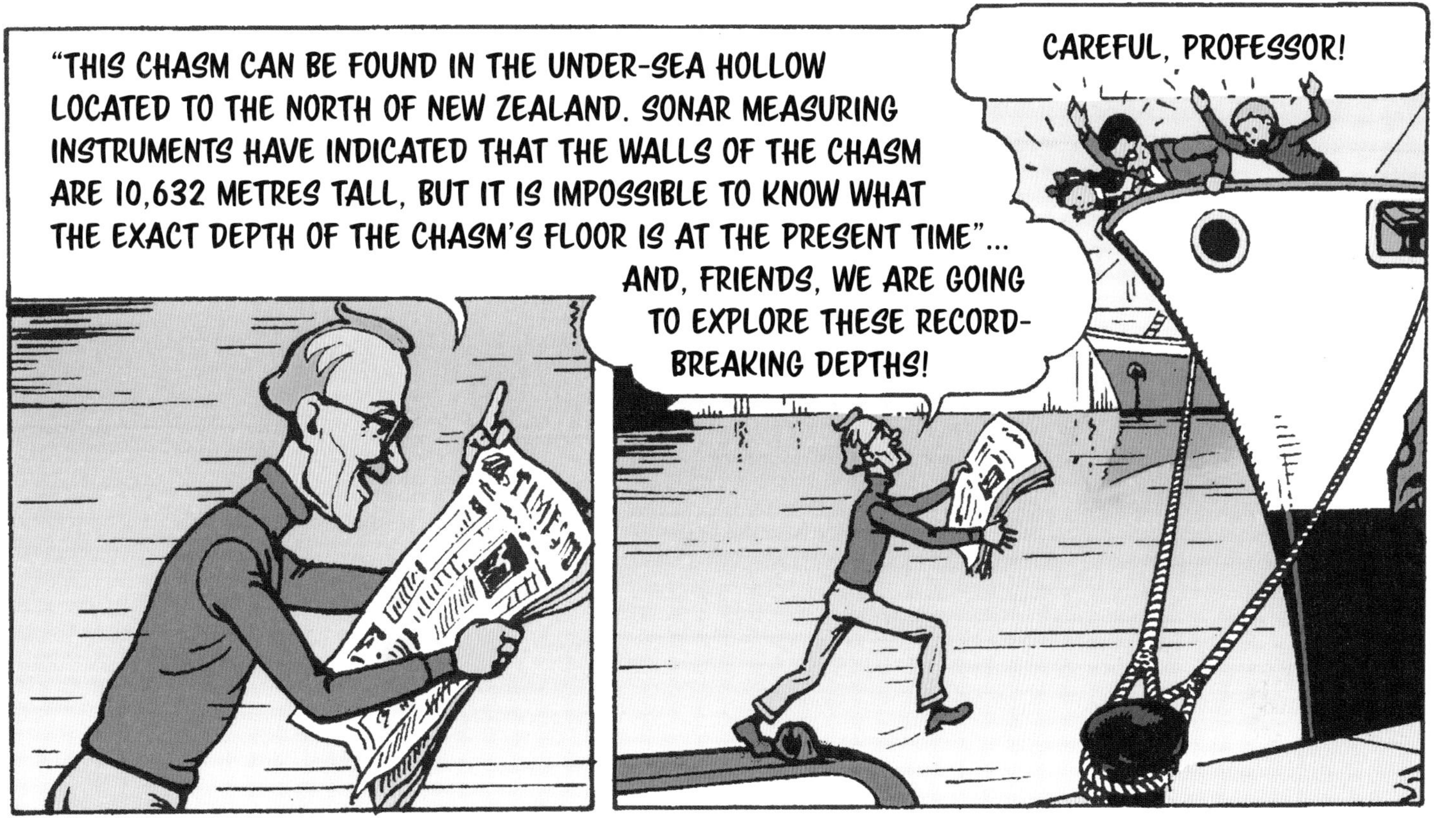
"THIS CHASM CAN BE FOUND IN THE UNDER-SEA HOLLOW LOCATED TO THE NORTH OF NEW ZEALAND. SONAR MEASURING INSTRUMENTS HAVE INDICATED THAT THE WALLS OF THE CHASM ARE 10,632 METRES TALL, BUT IT IS IMPOSSIBLE TO KNOW WHAT THE EXACT DEPTH OF THE CHASM'S FLOOR IS AT THE PRESENT TIME"...
TIMES
AND, FRIENDS, WE ARE GOING TO EXPLORE THESE RECORD-BREAKING DEPTHS!
CAREFUL, PROFESSOR!

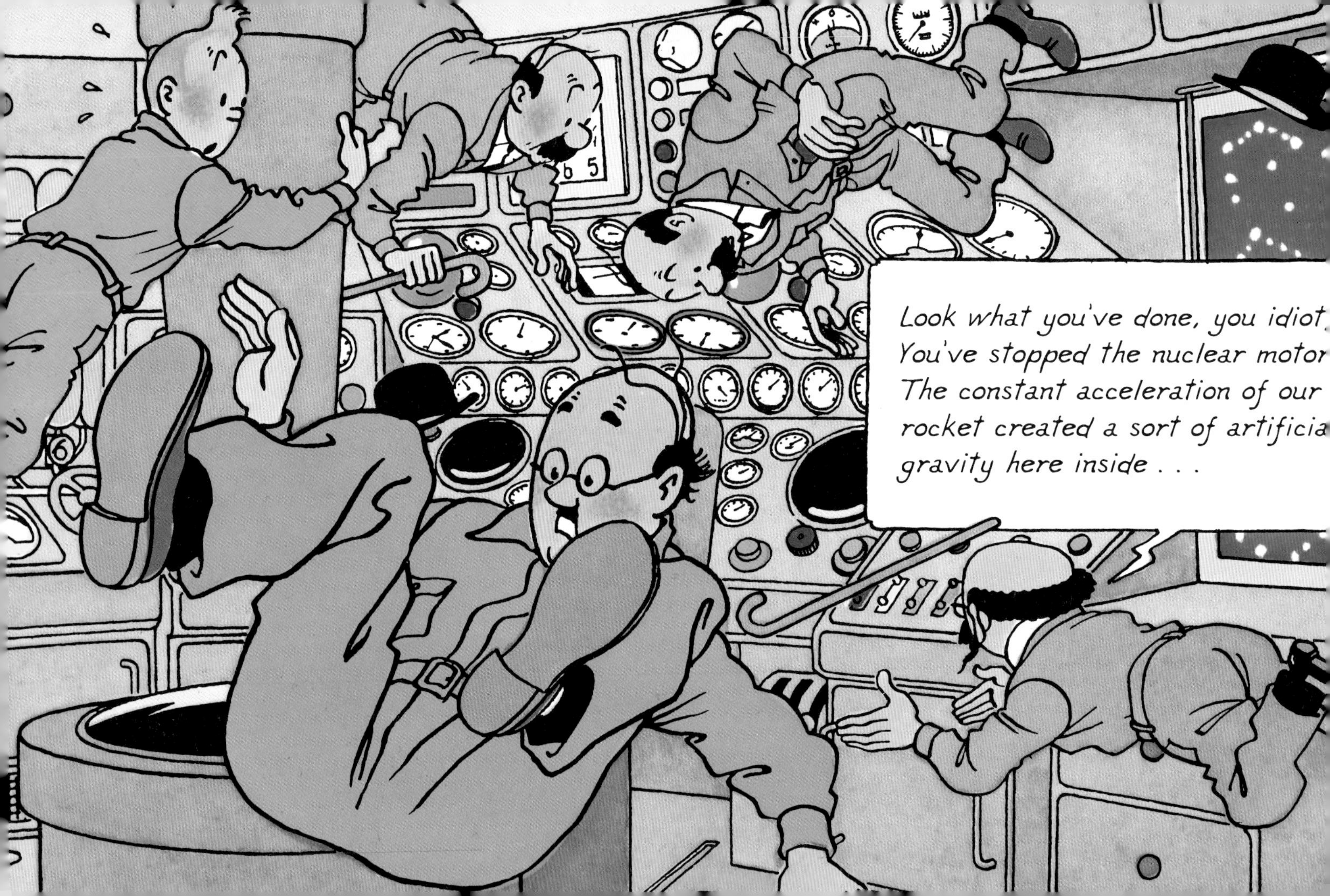
Look what you've done, you idiot You've stopped the nuclear motor The constant acceleration of our rocket created a sort of artificia gravity here inside . . .

A hugely knowledgeable man, Calculus is not content to master and develop a single scientific field. Whereas the consistency of knowledge between people poses problems for science and leads to specialisation, for Calculus, the unity of knowledge is no problem at all. Unlike the scholars who came after him, all of them specialists, he is a true jack of all trades, and a master of all.

CALCULUS: JACK OF ALL TRADES

Below is a comprehensive list of the scientific disciplines practised by Professor Calculus.

Astronautics:
the science and engineering of navigating in space. (*Explorers on the Moon, Destination Moon*).

Astronomy:
the science studying the position, structure, movements and development of celestial bodies. (*Explorers on the Moon*, p. 4, 10).

Astrophysics:
the part of astronomy studying the composition, physical properties and development of celestial bodies. (*Explorers on the Moon*, p. 7, 6 and 7; p. 32, 6).

Biology:
the science of life and, more specifically, the study of the reproductive cycle of living organisms. (*Tintin and the Picaros*, p. 38, 6).

Chemistry:
the science studying the atomic and molecular composition of bodies and their interactions. Together, the disciplines of nuclear chemistry, inorganic chemistry and applied chemistry cover the applications of chemistry in industry and pharmaceutics. Magnetochemistry and thermochemistry are also part of Calculus's repertoire. (*Destination Moon*, p. 16, 3, 4, 5; *Land of Black Gold*, p. 62, 5).

Classical Mechanics:
the science with the purpose of studying forces and movements. It has three main branches:
Statistics: the study of the action of forces on bodies in the absence of movement.
Kinematics:
the study of space, time and movements independent of their cause.
Dynamics:
the study of movements under the action of forces. (*The Red Sea Sharks*, p. 29, 9, 10, 11; p. 61, 3, 4, 5, 6).

Electroacoustics:
the technology of producing transmissions of recordings and of reproducing acoustic signals by electronic means. (*The Castafiore Emerald*, p. 48 to 50).

Electromechanical engineering:
all applications of electricity to mechanical engineering. (*Red Rackham's Treasure*, p. 8, 6).

Electronics:
the part of physics and engineering studying and using variations in electronic outputs to capture and transmit information. (*The Castafiore Emerald*, p. 48 to 50).

Geodetics:
the science of the shape and size of the Earth and of the Moon. (*Destination Moon, Explorers on the Moon*).

Geology:
the science with the purpose of describing the materials that constitute the Earth and studying the current and past transformations the Earth (and the Moon) have undergone. (*Explorers on the Moon*).

Geometry:
the mathematical science studying the relationships between points, lines, curves, surfaces and volumes of space.

Gravimetry:
the part of geodetics with the purpose of measuring gravitational force. (*Explorers on the Moon*, p. 6, 3 and 4).

Mathematics:
the science studying the properties of abstract entities (numbers, geometric shapes, functions, areas, etc.) as well as the relationships established between them, by means of deductive reasoning.

Metrology:
the science of measurements. (*Explorers on the Moon*, p. 32, 6).

Oceanography:
the physical, chemical and biological study of marine waters and the seabed. (*Red Rackham's Treasure*, p. 33, 4).

Physics:
the science studying the general properties of matter, space and time and establishing laws that account for natural phenomena.

Nuclear Physics:
the study of the forces and structure of atomic nuclei. (*Explorers on the Moon*, p. 16, 3, 4, 5).

The prone position is directly relevant to reactive aviation and to astronautics, as it enabled pilots to withstand high acceleration more comfortably. Alexandre Ananoff, *L'astronautique*, Librairie Arthème Fayard, 1950.

Phytotherapy:
the treatment of illness with plants. (*Tintin and the Picaros*, p. 42, 3, 5).

Thermodynamics:
the part of physics dealing with the relationships between mechanical and thermal phenomena. (*Red Rackham's Treasure*, p. 6, 10).

Zoology:
the branch of natural sciences studying animals. (*Tintin and the Picaros*, p. 38, 6).

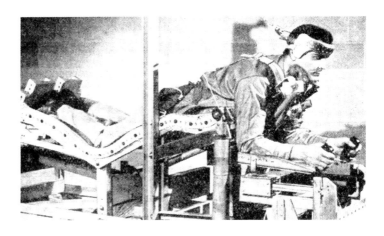

LABORATORIES

Just imagine! For the first time in history, cameras are now photographing the side of the Moon no one has ever seen! And it's thanks to us, my dear Wolff! Thanks to us!

For the man of science, there is no need for distant journeys if he wants to "dive into the unknown to find something new,"[14] because adventure awaits him inside his lab!

The professor's first laboratory is located in the uncomfortable attic to which Tintin, Haddock and the Thompson Twins make an eventful visit, to say the least (*Red Rackham's Treasure*, p. 6, 7, 8).

Once settled in Marlinspike Hall, the professor initially set up his laboratory in the Hall itself, on the ground floor of the right wing of the house. After the major explosion resulting from his experiments with N. 14 (*Land of Black Gold*, p. 62), the professor, strongly encouraged by Tintin and Captain Haddock, moved his laboratory into a separate building in the Hall's grounds, due to safety concerns. (*The Calculus Affair*, p. 14, 7).

At the Sprodj Atomic Research Centre, the professor enjoyed the benefits of facilities designed for the Moon Project.

In the rocket itself, he set up a laboratory that was in operation throughout the expedition. (*Destination Moon*, p. 44, 5).

14. The Voyage, Baudelaire.

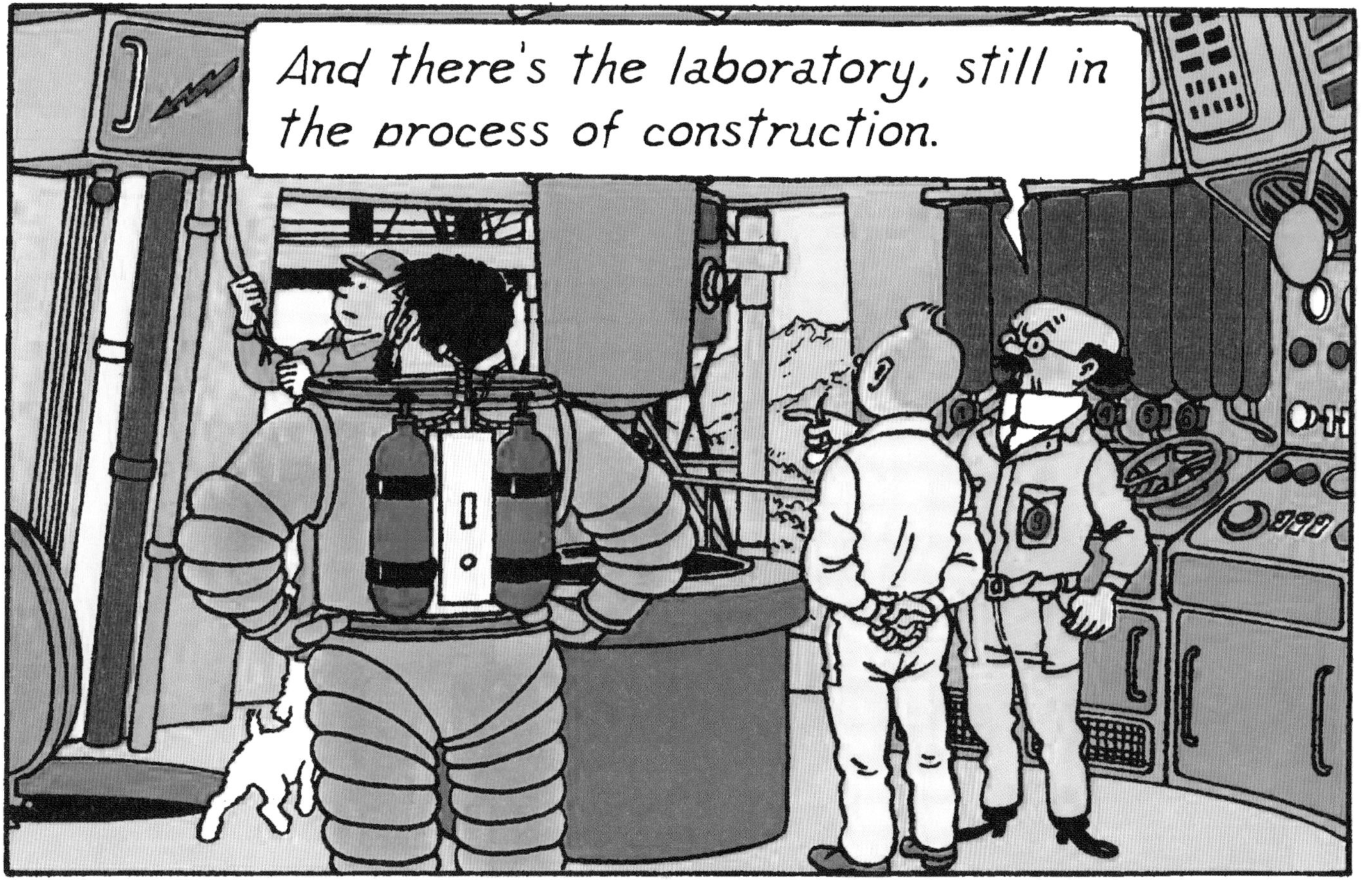
And there's the laboratory, still in the process of construction.

According to some sources, Calculus supposedly offered this gasogene-powered, front-wheel drive car to one of his young assistants with a large family.

Throughout his career, Calculus implements his knowledge  through his inventions: he moves from pure science to applied science.

CALCULUS'S INVENTIONS

The variety of Calculus's inventions affirms the extraordinary homogeneity of his knowledge and illustrates the highly poetic simplicity of Hergé's vision of progress. This progress does not occur in short bounds, but rather occurs steadily over time.

From his clothes-brushing machine to the moon rocket, and to finally amazing Bianca Castafiore with his rose, who would doubt Calculus's genius for innovation?

It therefore makes sense to sort Calculus's inventions in chronological order.

A new gasogene (a device for producing gas)

A gasogene is a device that converts coal or wood into combustible gas by means of complete oxidation.

During the Second World War, Calculus was able to help some of his friends who were having difficulties due to petrol rationing, by fitting his new gasogene device to their cars.

Like other gasogenes, Calculus's device produced a lean gas by burning wood or charcoal, or even coke or anthracite.

However, what made it original was its compact size in comparison to other very bulky devices that couldn't be integrated into car bodies, but instead had to be fixed to the roof at the back or at the front of the vehicle, and that furthermore could not be fitted to engines of small cars.

Not only did Calculus succeed in reducing this encumbrance by decreasing the size of the furnace, the filters, the compressor and the fittings, he also managed to equip less-powerful vehicles with the device. With the liberation of France, petrol was no longer in short supply and this put an end to the hopes aroused by this invention.

Yes, that's a new device for putting bubbles in soda-water . . .

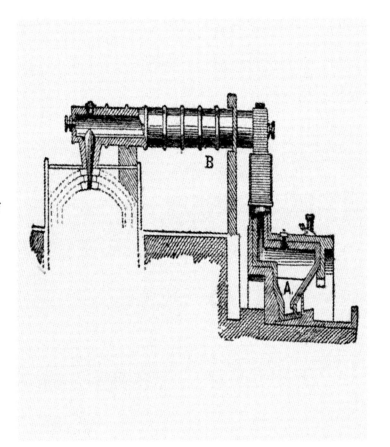

A clothes-brushing machine

Although rather unwieldy, quite noisy, of questionable looks and not suitable for all fabric types, the clothes-brushing machine invented by the professor is formidably efficient.

Calculus succeeded in selling the patent to some manufacturers who, by reducing the size of this device, knew how to make it into a classic household appliance.

Traditional clothes brushes

Reduced-size electronic brush inspired by Calculus's brushing machine

A wall bed

Calculus's disregard for his own comfort and the cramped conditions of his flat account for the creation of the wall bed, which consists of a bed frame that folds away into the wall by means of a mechanism operated by a lever.

When the baby-boom of the post-war years caused space problems for large families housed in overcrowded homes, the professor's invention inspired several interior designer-decorators.

...signed the wall-bed.

"Built-in" beds inspired by
Calculus's wall bed.

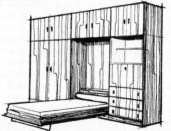

Woody Rigsby's Nautilette, a later imitation of Calculus's submarine, appeared in *Popular Mechanics March 1962.*

The shark submarine

Calculus's shark-shaped submersible is fast and gives its pilot a clear view. It is fitted with an electric propeller engine, powered by downsized batteries, equipped with oxygen tanks allowing self-sufficient dives of up to two hours. Shortly after Calculus's invention, in 1948, the Italian Pietro Vassena developed an allegedly pocket-sized submarine that was 7.5m long and 1.5m in diameter.

It wasn't until 1957 that Count Champignac[15] devised a somewhat more high-performance craft, followed in 1960 by Major Cousteau and his diving saucer Sp350. In 1962, the American Woody Rigsby launched the *Nautilette*, a two-seater submarine capable of a five-hour trip.

15. See Le repaire de la Murène. (The Moray's Keep). Dupuis 1957.

The counteragent for N. 14

When Calculus analyses the substance N. 14 at the end of *Land of Black Gold*, he discovers that if you "add only a minute part to petrol its explosive qualities are increased to an alarming degree" (*Land of Black Gold*, p. 61).

A "great foreign power" intended to use this substance on a large scale, to make their rivals' fuel supplies unusable. Calculus, having analysed the product, solving the mystery of the explosive engines, finds the answer by devising a counteragent capable of counteracting the effects of N. 14.

Thomson and Thompson had the terrible idea of taking tablets from an aspirin bottle mislaid by Doctor Müller to cure their headaches. The effects of N. 14 on these two involuntary guinea pigs didn't take long to show: they immediately began to suffer from the growth of huge amounts of hair (hyperpilosity) and a disorder changing the colouring of their hair. Once more, Calculus finds the antidote to cure the unfortunate pair. It is a treatment he has to prescribe to them again

after a particularly bad relapse they suffered during the lunar expedition (*Explorers on the Moon*, p. 12-34).

The experimental rocket X-FLR 6

The X-FLR 6 was a smaller model of the lunar rocket used to go to the Moon, intended to take photos of the dark side of the Moon and radio-controlled from the Sprodj Atomic Research Centre. This would have been a first for both astronomy and astronautics, if a foreign power's radio control station had not intercepted the signals to hijack the rocket and take it off course. Calculus was forced to blow it up to prevent it falling into the wrong hands.

It was not until October 1959 that the Soviet probe Luna 3 successfully transmitted the first photos of the dark side of the Moon to Earth. (*Destination Moon*, p. 15 and 29).

The Lunar Rocket

This was constructed using fifteen different major components and powered by an atomic engine. The Lunar Rocket can be seen as the successor of several machines, such as Allemand Oberth's *Cosmoney* and Zolkowsky's *Astronef*.

By landing his rocket on the Moon or on the Earth, using a turning operation triggered by turning on engines giving directional thrust, Calculus showed that it was possible for the same single-stage rocket to launch into space and to return to

Earth in the same position in which it left, namely upright.

By making light of these supposedly insurmountable problems, the professor once again showed the great extent to which he was ahead of his Russian and American counterparts, who opted to employ the principle of multistage combustion-powered rockets.

However, in 1991, the McDonnell Douglas firm, inspired by the work of Professor Calculus, began studying the idea of a reusable single-stage rocket on behalf of the Pentagon, and in 1993 successful trials were conducted on the White Sands Missile Range.

Le Parisien libéré,

The Pentagon tests Tintin's Rocket

A single-stage rocket that takes off and lands upright... the first trials have taken place in the deserts of

It seems as if Hergé, like Jules Verne before him, had a point: we could go to space tomorrow and return to Earth with the same single-stage rocket, which would land on home soil in the same position as that in which it left: upright.

The trials of this revolutionary rocket, the Delta Clipper Experimental (DC-X) are currently being conducted in the New Mexican desert by the American firm McDonnell Douglas. These have the potential to transform future spacecraft launches by dramatically simplifying the methods used.

All those who directly assisted with the moon landing on the 20th of July 1969, which put Neil Armstrong's LEM on the Moon, were struck by the extraordinary similarity between their achievement and the storyline conceived several years before by the Father of Tintin. That is, except for one little detail: the astronauts actually had to move into the Lunar

on Wednesday enabled the twelve-metre-tall Delta-Clipper to climb forty-five metres into the air and to return to the launchpad, after a lateral flight of about a hundred metres. A second flight reaching two hundred metres is scheduled for the 27th of August.

The first challenge of a rocket such as this one is economic: simplifying launches and saving making stages that are dropped in space should reduce costs significantly: according to McDonnell, the Delta-Clipper costs just ten million dollars, whereas launching a space shuttle costs four hundred and nine million dollars.

But the technological requirements are just as complicated, particularly in terms of saving on weight.

On this topic, the American firm has speculated that by 1998, rockets with a height of thirty-eight metres could be carrying a load of up to eleven tonnes into orbit.

The rocket from "Destination Moon" and from "Explorers on the Moon": Hergé described Tintin, Snowy, Captain Haddock and Professor Calculus's exploration of the Queen of the night sky at the start of the nineteen-fifties. The

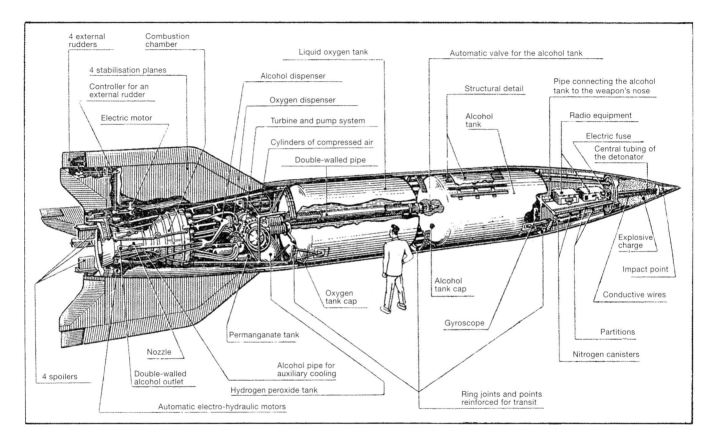

4 external rudders

Combustion chamber

4 stabilisation planes

Controller for an external rudder

Electric motor

Liquid oxygen tank

Alcohol dispenser

Oxygen dispenser

Turbine and pump system

Cylinders of compressed air

Double-walled pipe

Automatic valve for the alcohol tank

Structural detail

Alcohol tank

Pipe connecting the alcohol tank to the weapon's nose

Radio equipment

Electric fuse

Central tubing of the detonator

Explosive charge

Impact point

Conductive wires

Partitions

Nitrogen canisters

Alcohol tank cap

Gyroscope

Oxygen tank cap

Permanganate tank

Nozzle

Double-walled alcohol outlet

Alcohol pipe for auxiliary cooling

Hydrogen peroxide tank

4 spoilers

Automatic electro-hydraulic motors

Ring joints and points reinforced for transit

The infamous V2 Rocket foreshadowed Calculus's aeronautical rocket. Drawing taken and translated from L'astronautique, Ananoff 1950.

Auxiliary Motors

In 1950, in his brilliant work L'astronautique, (Astronautics), Alexandre Ananoff, referring to the problems with atomic drive for space rockets, proposed that "firstly the rocket's take-off into the first layers of our atmosphere, secondly its landing" are achieved "using a force that goes against the direction of travel, created by auxiliary flares using liquid rocket fuel."[16] This is to avoid the real radiation storm that the rocket's nuclear reactors would undoubtedly cause during the rocket's acceleration or deceleration. Not long after this, Professor Calculus, aware that "a radioactive blast from the exhausts would be a frightful hazard at the launching and landing sites," provided a masterful solution to the problem raised by Ananoff, using "another engine, a simple jet using a mixture of nitric acid and aniline" specifically "for launching and landing." (*Destination Moon*, p. 16, 4).

Of course, for launching and landing we shall use another engine, a simple jet, using a mixture of nitric acid and aniline . . . Why? . . . Because if we used the nuclear motor then, the radioactive blast from the exhausts . . .

. . . would be a frightful hazard at the launching and landing sites . . . You may argue that the intense heat engendered by the nuclear fission would melt the motor itself! No! Because I have invented a new substance, calculon. It has a silicon base, and can resist even the highest temperatures. Thanks to these two inventions - the nuclear motor and calculon - we shall soon set foot on the Moon.

Calculon

Calculon is a silicone-based substance that is completely indispensable for the atomic engine, as it is designed to resist the highest temperatures in order to prevent the extreme heat produced by radioactive decay melting the lunar rocket's engine.

Great scientists and famous inventors are often given the privilege of having one of their discoveries named after them.

Thus, with Calculon, Calculus joins the ranks of those such as Baekeland and Bakelite, Diesel and the diesel engine, Pasteur and pasteurisation, Sax and the saxophone, Phostle and phostlite, etc.

16. Alexandre Ananoff, *L'astronautique*, Librarire Arthème Fayard, 1950.

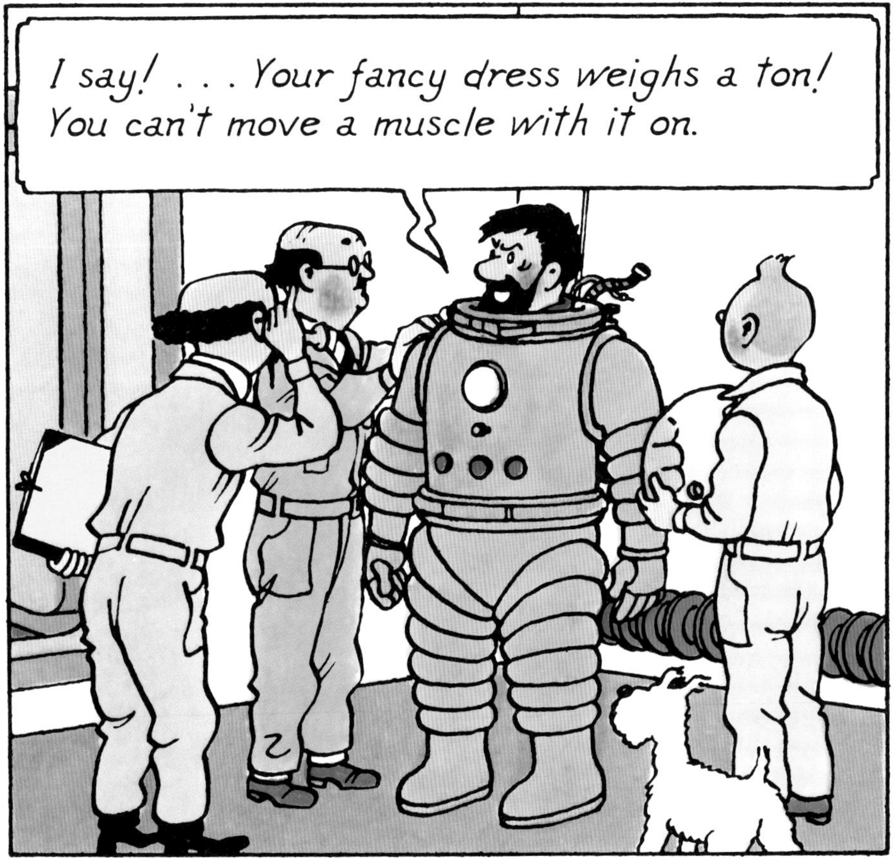
I say! . . . Your fancy dress weighs a ton! You can't move a muscle with it on.

The lunar spacesuit

Building on his oceanographic and manometric experiments, which allowed him to perfect his oxygen supply device for his submarine, Calculus had no difficulty designing the first self-contained lunar spacesuit, equipped with a radio and a Plexiglas helmet (*Destination Moon*, p. 36).

Admittedly research into spacesuits had previously been undertaken. Here, we can mention the spacesuit tested by Swain (an Englishman) in 1936, in an aeroplane that had ascended to 15,230m altitude; the Italian Pezzi's spacesuit, tested in 1937; or even the apparatus made by the Frenchman Richou in 1942. However, Calculus was the first to solve all the problems posed by the development of a lunar spacesuit, whether that of resisting the pressure of existing in a vacuum, of cosmic and ultraviolet radiation, or even that of its bulk and of making it self-contained. Snowy's spacesuit required specialised development due to his canine body shape. Despite the progress subsequently made in space research in both the United States and in the USSR, the astronauts from these two countries never benefitted from spacesuits as space efficient as those designed by Professor Calculus.

Collapsible vehicle able to carry two astronauts and their equipment. It was used during the Apollo missions 15, 16 and 17.

The lunar tank

Twenty-six years before the Soviets were remotely operating the *Lunokhod* (a vehicle with eight wheels that took and transmitted more than 20,000 photos back to Earth) on the surface of the Moon, Calculus

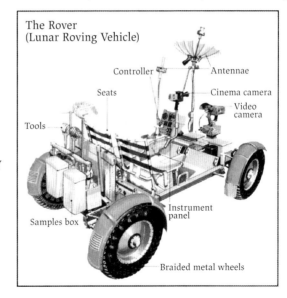

The Rover
(Lunar Roving Vehicle)

Controller
Antennae
Seats
Cinema camera
Video camera
Tools
Instrument panel
Samples box
Braided metal wheels

invented the lunar tank (*Explorers on the Moon*, p. 32 to 38).

The first to drive it was Tintin, who reminisces about this in *The Calculus Affair*, while having great difficulty driving a Bordurian tank (*The Calculus Affair*, p. 59, 9).

An ultrasound transmitter

Taking inspiration from the work of German scientists who attempted to use ultrasound for destructive purposes during the Second World War, Calculus managed to design the ultimate weapon, more powerful than the atom bomb or the hydrogen bomb, and able to destroy entire towns from a great distance.

Calculus was kidnapped on the orders of Marshal Kûrvi-Tasch, who wanted to put this weapon to use in the expansionist activities of the great major state of Borduria, at which point Syldavian secret service agents had also already tried to capture him. Fortunately, once rescued by Haddock and Tintin, the professor decided to destroy the microfilm plans for this wicked weapon.

However, an incomplete copy of these plans was stolen in the Bordurian state offices by a member of the secret moustachist police, Stefan Szhrinkoff, a double agent working on behalf of the Belgradian secret services.

After several years of work, researchers for the Serbian armed forces managed to finalise the ultrasound weapon Calculus invented. It is also relevant to note here that Calculus was a student of the mathematician Eugène Mathieu.

Liberation Newspaper, January 1994

The Serbian Secret Weapon, according to Zhirinovsky

This "secret weapon" with which the Serbain forces in Bosnia are being provided is apparently known as Elipton, and the ultra-nationalist Russian leader Vladimir Zhirinovsky, whose latest visit to ex-Yugoslavia ended just yesterday, is claiming that this is no laughing matter: "Russian counter-espionage officers used the weapon against a military unit on Wednesday, killing 12 enemy soldiers. Their dead bodies showed no trace of firearm injuries and the surrounding buildings were not damaged."

Elipton supposedly kills using certain types of ultrasound. This story might seem absurd, and some of Zhirinovsky's close political allies are attempting to downplay this statement, however Zhirinovsky is insistent, condemning those who are sceptical and "all those who fear the Party's power and the might of the new Russia." Some of the Serbian press is adding their spin on this, citing academics with grand titles who maintain that the concept of this revolutionary weapon, that is capable of inverting the existing power balance with the West, is supposedly based on the work of a nineteenth-century French mathematician: Eugène Mathieu.

S. Etr

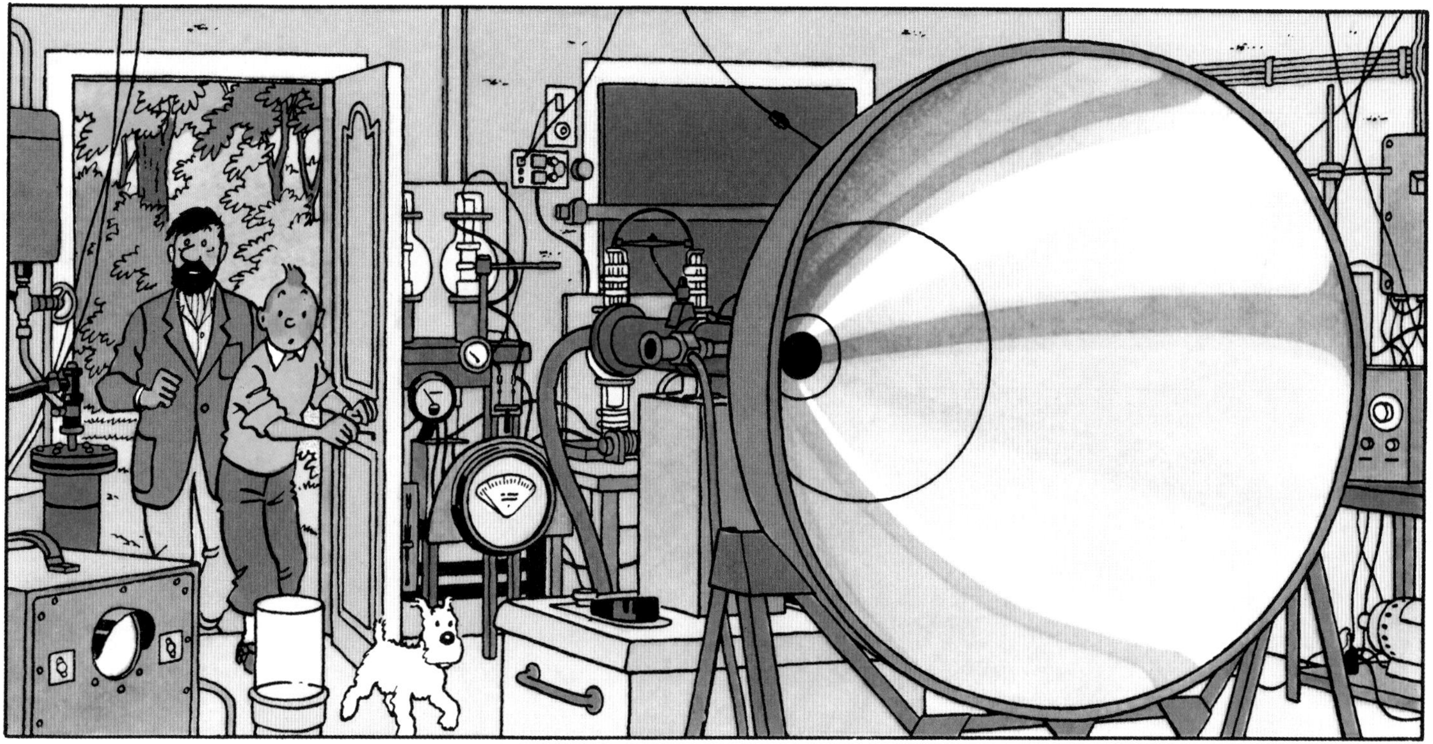

After *The Calculus Affair*,
the professor returns to
inventions reminiscent of
his early days as an inventor.
As we see with Phostle in
The Shooting Star, Calculus
understands the importance
of distancing himself in time
from the knowledge that
threatens to possess him.
He displays scruples that
show that science has not
suppressed his conscience.
"It's everyone who wants to
use my invention for warlike
ends. And I shall never allow
that." (*The Calculus Affair*,
p. 62, 4).

At least motorised roller
skates, the Super-Calcacolor,
the Bianca Castafiore rose
and anti-alcohol tablets can't
hurt anyone. At least, in
theory.

Roller skates with motorised wheels

Throughout *The Red Sea Sharks*, the invention of motorised roller skates is a project that occupies Calculus's mind. When challenged by Haddock, who is astonished by Calculus's use of such a singular mode of transport for joining them for breakfast, Calculus remains cryptic: "I can't tell you anything more at present..." (*The Red Sea Sharks*, p. 8).

Later, with Tintin and Haddock having left for Khemed, the professor returns to Marlinspike Hall's kitchen to ask Nestor to give him a little push. This time, he has fitted a type of steering comparable to that used for steering toy cars to his roller skates. It is on this occasion that Abdallah inflicts an unintended rotating experience on him, simultaneously subjecting all the kitchen utensils to the effects of a particularly destructive centrifugal force (*The Red Sea Sharks*, p. 29).

Calculus crashes into Tintin, Snowy and Haddock on a garden path upon their return to Marlinspike while travelling at high speed on his finalised roller skates. Fitted with four wheels and a 28cm³ two-stroke engine controlled by hoses that enable both adjusting the throttle and steering, the skates can reach a speed of 40 miles an hour (*The Red Sea Sharks*, p. 61).

Although Calculus has, with these roller skates, found an ideal solution to tackle the problem of vehicular traffic in overly congested towns, it is surprising that no local government has ever contacted him to test this affordable, if somewhat embarrassing, mode of transport.

In March 1966, this photo appeared in French magazine Science et Vie: "Your roller skates can become a mode of transport. Simply fit a small, air-cooled engine with manually-controlled acceleration and breaking. And the petrol tank? You can carry this on your back." The same year, having bought Calculus's patent, the American firm Motorized Roller Skate Co., tried to commercialise roller skates with motorised wheels.

Motor-roller-skates. For a long time I've been trying to find an answer to the traffic problem . . . I was thinking of a flexible, handy, lightweight machine . . . ?

A black and white telecinema experience conducted in 1936. The professor needed almost 30 years to succeed with colour.

The Super-Calcacolor

Contrary to what Calculus announces to his friends when he is preparing to give them a demonstration of the colour television device he has developed in his laboratory, the moment is not an "historic" one (*The Castafiore Emerald*, p. 48).

Certainly, the imagined principle – "colour filters inserted between an ordinary television set and a special screen" – is ingenious, but in Great Britain another scientist, John L. Baird (1888-1946) had already conducted tests for a colour television on 1st July 1928, well before Calculus.

The first public television programmes were broadcast by CBS in New York starting in 1951, which Captain Haddock seems to know, but

his remark that "You know, someone has already..." is interrupted by yet another misunderstanding à la Calculus. Calculus can therefore not be legitimately considered to be a pioneer in the context of the invention of the colour television. The

fact remains that his work influenced that of French researchers in 1963, the year when he developed the Super-Calcacolor.

With the advent of the Field-sequential colour system in the USA by Dr Peter Goldmark, Super-

Calcacolor was rendered obselete, and Professor Calculus abandoned it.

The Bianca Castafiore Rose

In the gardens of Marlinspike Hall, Calculus managed to cultivate a new variety of rose. This was the fruit of time-consuming and patient horticultural work, the idea for which came to him while visiting the Chelsea Flower Show (*The Castafiore Emerald*, p. 23). As a tribute to the renowned opera singer, Calculus christens this new white rose the "Bianca Castafiore."

As if the symbolism of this floral, colour-based analogy (Calculus offering a white rose to the *Chaste Flower* who also plays Marguerite – meaning daisy – in Gounod's *Faust*...) were not enough, it also happens that in the language of flowers, a white rose symbolises silence!

The anti-alcohol tablets

A tasteless, odourless and non-toxic product prepared from medicinal herbs, this remarkable repellent comes in tablet form. When dissolved into a drink or food, a single one of these pills makes all alcohol subsequently consumed taste terrible.

It is when he is used as a guinea pig by the professor without his knowledge that Haddock temporarily gives up whisky. Thanks to this medication, the Arumbayas and then the Picaros avoid relapsing into alcoholism.

Since these promising experiments, the Society of Sober Sailors – of which Haddock is the Honorary President – has funded Professor Calculus's research in view of commercialising this pill on a large scale.

IT ABOUNDS IN OUR COUNTRY

The anti-alcohol mushroom

A mushroom, the common inkcap to be precise, could be remarkably effective in combatting alcoholism, especially for curing unapologetic drinkers.

This fungus grows abundantly in Switzerland and it is well known by mushroom hunters and appreciated by connoisseurs. Harmless and delicious, it does however cause very unpleasant side effects if, after having eaten it, you consume alcohol within 48 hours of ingestion. A tankard of beer or a glass of wine is all it takes to cause poisoning that results in reddening of the face, hot flushes and vomiting. This poisoning is, however, not very severe.

Recently, a group of Swedish chemists led by Professor Wickberg was urged to isolate the substance from the mushroom that produces the anti-alcoholic reaction and to explain its chemical structure. The substance – coprine – inhibits the body's metabolism of alcohol, which in turn increases the level of ethanal (acetaldehyde) in the blood, leading to the blood poisoning symptoms noted here.

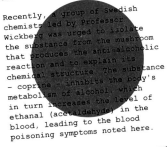

In conclusion, another huge thank you for the article from the Lausanne Tribune. You have worked out that it was clearly from the "common inkcap" (the existence of which I was unaware of) that Professor Calculus made his anti-alcohol tablets!

Best wishes

On 7th February 1976, an article from the *Lausanne Tribune* implied the medicinal herb from which Calculus developed his anti-alcohol tablet was the *inkcap mushroom*, a very prevalent mushroom in Switzerland. It should be noted that this information dates from the exact time (February 1976) when Calculus was undertaking his experiments. This suggestion sent by Alain Talma, an eminent Tintin expert, was confirmed by Hergé himself.

On 30th November 1911 in Brussels, an international conference on "radiation theory and quanta" brought together the most eminent scholars, including Planck, Marie Curie, Poincaré, Langevin and the young Einstein. Calculus, who had not heard that the meeting had started, unfortunately does not feature in this souvenir photo.

During his very long career, Professor Cuthbert

Calculus mixed with the most prestigious scientists.

EMINENT COLLEAGUES

SCIENTISTS WHO WERE MEMBERS OF THE SANDERS-HARDMUTH EXPEDITION

Tarragon (Hercules)
Calculus undertook all his studies with Hercules Tarragon who, like him, has a name associated with a plant (in the French original), and a Greek first name. An eminent Americanist, Tarragon participated in the Sanders-Hardmuth expedition in this capacity, and Rascar Capac's mummy is kept in his house.

It is therefore not

surprising that he was the seventh victim of the Inca's curse.

Cantonneau (Paul)
See page 30.

Hornet
The director of the Natural History Museum. The door to his office was guarded by the Thompsons when a crystal ball, thrown in via the window, also plunges him into a slumber from which he can only be roused by the destruction of the image that represents him.

Laubépin
A professor whose specialism is not known, he is also a victim of the mysterious crystal balls.

Sanders-Hardmuth
The head of the expedition that bears his name, he is the second to be struck by the Inca's curse, after the filmmaker Clairmont.

Baxter

The director of the Sprodj Atomic Research Centre in Syldavia. Originally from the United States, Baxter returns to his home country in 1967 so as to benefit American astronautics with the experience he gained working alongside Professor Calculus.

N° 31

On 28th December 1987, following the publication of the book *Tintinolâtrie*, Hergé's publisher Casterman received a mysterious letter signed 'Gagarinovitch.'

Having been properly authenticated, this letter was able to shed light on an associate of Professor Calculus, codenamed N° 31.

In 1950, I was responsible, under the direct authority of C. Calculus, for the "Lunar Equipment" division, and more specifically for the development of the lunar spacesuit, at the Sprodj Atomic Research Centre that is nowadays so well-known. Mr Hergé had the utmost courtesy to depict me acting in this capacity on pages 7 and 8 of Destination Moon: my name will mean nothing to you, but I was N° 31 in the centre's organisational structure, which wasn't nothing, since Mr. Baxter was N° 1, C. Calculus N° 9, F. Wolff N° 14, and Messrs Haddock and Tintin were only 56 and 57, respectively.

I was recruited at the same time as F. Wolff, who I had met at White Sands (USA). This background earned me some serious grief after the rocket's return and the distressing events that accompanied this. In fact, at the start of the 50s, the mood of the times in Syldavia reflected undertones of McCarthyism, to which I fell victim.

The colleagues and friends of F. Wolff were suspected of having participated in Colonel Boris, aka Jorgen's, illicit embarkation: you will remember that the Bordurian spy had entered the rocket, in a box from the Jena Optical Plant in the German Democratic Republic. F. Wolff was responsible for sourcing provisions and equipment, and my duties had been completed at this time. I believe I took the rap for the men of the Zepo, who were unable to effectively control access to Sbrodj or even to the rocket — look at how the two policemen Thomson and Thompson managed to board the rocket!

I was criticised for trifles that did not justify, in my opinion, my expulsion from the Centre. For example, the incident of Snowy's spacesuit was brought up again. Too large for him, the suit would have fitted a Saint Bernard. I had only followed C. Calculus's instructions, who knew Mr Tintin's dog well. Similarly, if Snowy got into the restricted access area dressed like that, the burden for this rests on F. Wolff, as he has acknowledged. During preliminary tests for A. Haddock's lunar spacesuit, I willingly recognise that it was I who forgot to remove the white mice that were used in the first experiments.

However, I have been far more unfairly reproached for having used Plexiglas for construction of the helmet of this same spacesuit, which C. Calculus and I tested ourselves with the most scientific and rigorous methods possible. In the hysterical, excessively anti-communist climate of this era, the reference to Plexiglas was not a politically neutral one in Syldavia, and regrettably sounded like an echo of appreciation for Kûrvi-Tasch (named Plekszy-Gladz in the French original), who was, at this time, number 1 in the Moustaschist party in power in Borduria.

This truly regrettable similarity in names was impossible to explain, and I was simply dismissed, before being forbidden from residing in Syldavia for the next ten years.

Gagarinovitch

Franck Wolff

Wolff's gambling addiction and the debts he accumulated caused him to fall prey to blackmailers. In his role as Calculus's senior assistant at the Sprodj plant, Wolff is forced into spying on then into betraying Calculus – he agrees to send the rocket blueprints to those who want to steal them, and most importantly, he brings a dangerous illicit passenger aboard the lunar ship: Boris Jorgen.

What the French playwright Jean Racine said of his character Phèdre, who, in his eyes, appeared "neither completely guilty, nor completely innocent,"[17] applies perfectly to Wolff.

Admittedly, this character suffers from the effects of a disastrous addiction, which causes him to no longer act as himself, but the guilt that is eating away at him shows that this scientist has a strong moral compass, torn between misconduct and repaying his debts, between disgrace and a clean conscience.

To escape from the burden of remorse, Wolff chooses to unburden himself by committing suicide in the weightlessness of outer space. This stunning gesture (*Explorers on the Moon*, p. 55, 3) redeems him in the eyes of those he had betrayed, while also saving their lives.

The redemptive significance of this death does not escape Tintin, who describes it as a "sacrifice" (*Explorers on the Moon*, p. 55, 6).

17. Racine, Phèdre, Preface.

Topolino (Alfredo)

This Swiss physicist and specialist in ultrasonics still lives at 57A, route de Saint-Cergue, Nyon (tel. 9.51.03). His house, which was almost entirely destroyed by a bomb, was rebuilt at the expense of the ambassador to Borduria, once the liability of his country's secret service in the attack was officially established.

113, route de St-Cergue: Professor Topolino's house, in its restored state. From the Swiss Newspaper ㉔ *Heures*, 9-10 January '93

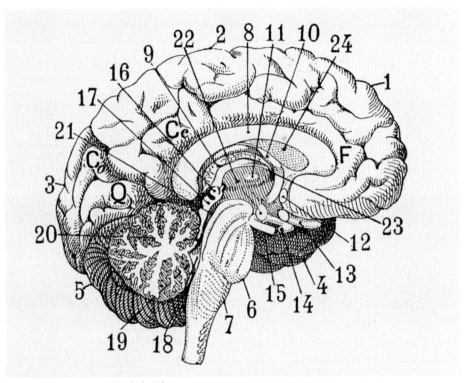

Longitudinal cross-section of Calculus's brain.
The incredible abilities of Professor Calculus's brain – from the frontal lobe (1) to the precuneus (Q) – cannot be detailed here. However, the unusual degeneration of the auditory nerve (4) can be noted.

If science is inhuman, then scientists have a duty to remain human, lest they succumb to delusions of grandeur or general madness.

Calculus is a human scientist par excellence, with his emotions, his feelings, his faults and his positive traits.

THE PSYCHOLOGY OF CALCULUS

Absent-mindedness

Calculus knows exactly where he stands regarding the judgements others pass on him: "Calculus is forever distracted, he never listens to what people are saying to him." "He always gives irrelevant answers to questions." "He's permanently in a world of his own."

However, if this all seems unfounded to him, (at the end of *The Calculus Affair*, p. 62, he exclaims "imagine me being so absent-minded"), it is true that absent-mindedness is one of the key traits of his character:

He uses the Captain's pipe as an ear trumpet (*Destination Moon*, p. 11, 10).

He throws away the lunar rocket blueprints and, in their place, locks some old newspapers in the safe (*Destination Moon*, p. 15).

He leaves the microfilms that he believed he had concealed in his umbrella on his bedside table (*The*

Calculus Affair, p, 62, 1).

Showered with whisky spat out by Haddock, he exclaims "I shouldn't have come without my umbrella" (*The Castafiore Emerald*, p. 7, 3).

He mistakes Castafiore for a painter and congratulates her on her pictures (The *Castafiore Emerald*, p. 9, 4).

He sits down on Snowy (*Tintin and the Picaros*, p. 14, 4) and takes a bath in his dressing gown (*Tintin and the Picaros*, p. 16, 12).

Clumsiness

This absent-mindedness is often accompanied by great clumsiness:

He bumps into a tree. (*The Seven Crystal Balls*, p. 39, 10).

This image could be considered a parallel with the one in which Sarcophagus bumps into the ship's airshaft. (*Cigars of the Pharoah*, p. 3, 11).

In *Destination Moon*, the professor shows himself to be the clumsiest of all, although he nevertheless plans to skilfully pilot the rocket to land on the Moon:

He injures Baxter with a stone that flies out of his ear trumpet. (*Destination Moon*, p. 18).

He inadvertently punches Haddock. (*Destination Moon*, p. 30, 2).

He forgets to remove his headphones. (*Destination Moon*, p. 32, 18).

He rips out some of Haddock's beard. (*Destination Moon*, p. 33, 12).

He shuts Haddock's head in a door. (*Destination Moon*, p. 52, 12).

He falls through an airlock hatch. (*Destination Moon*, p. 45, 14 and 15).

He burns the Captain's beard when setting fire to the

microfilms. (*The Calculus Affair*, p, 62, 6).

He can't stay upright on his roller skates, with or without a motor. (*The Red Sea Sharks*, p. 8, 7 and p. 61, 3).

Ridiculous blindness

As was the case with Professor Phostle, Calculus's extreme rationality can suddenly turn into complete irrationality.

In this way, the professor contemplates that he and his companions could be "completely pulverised" by the meteorite heading straight for them with an air of the greatest calm.

For him too, the scientific examination of the situation outweighs the possible disastrous consequences of it, and, oblivious to the incoherence in his reasoning,

he continues: "But don't worry! We'll soon know!" (*Explorers on the Moon*, p. 14, 8).

If he later demonstrates great emotion and if he confesses to having been scared, it's not at all for the same reasons as for Tintin and Haddock, who thought their time was up, but rather because, as he ridiculously explains: "if my theories hadn't worked out, I'd have had to begin all my calculations over again." (*Explorers on the Moon*, p. 15).

Equally bizarrely, when the crucial stage of the rocket's moon landing begins, Calculus exclaims: "Just think: in a few minutes' time, either we'll be walking on the Moon, or we'll all be dead. It's marvellous!" (*Explorers on the Moon*, p. 20).

Anger

Though he often remains very calm and almost indifferent to what is happening around him – a placidness that is in fact linked to his deafness – Calculus can be susceptible to remarkable fits of rage. However, we have to wait until preparations for the lunar expedition are underway for the outbursts to arise that turn him into a real typhoon.

He tears his hair out because the test rocket is in danger of falling into enemy hands (*Destination Moon*, p. 33, 11).

Most notably, he flies into an incontrollable rage when Haddock talks about him acting the "goat" (*Destination Moon*, p. 39 to 49).

At the start of *The Red Sea Sharks*, when Haddock repeats this idea (p. 9, 2): "Haven't you finished acting the goat yet?", the professor remains unreactive, but in *Flight 714 to Sydney* (p. 7, 9, 10), he reacts very badly when Haddock is foolish enough to comment "Isn't it time you stopped acting the goat?" Calculus's rages are as violent as they are sudden, triggering startling changes in his tone or attitude (*Explorers on the Moon*, p. 19, 11, 12; *Flight 714 to Sydney*, p. 49, 13).

When he loses his temper, unlike Haddock, the professor's language remains mild. Even during the terrible rage the Captain provokes in *Destination Moon*, except for "you worm!" an insult he directs at a guard refusing to let him pass and for "stars above" (*Destination Moon*, p. 45, 7), an expression so old that it can be found in the 1832 novella Le colonel Chabert by the French author Balzac, there is none of the colourful swearing that enlivens Haddock's rages.

The expletives Calculus uses are all similar to those Tintin uses, for example "well I never!" and "confound it!" (*Destination Moon*, p. 11, 11 and p. 32, 13); "great sunspots!" (*The Castafiore Emerald* p. 23, 7) and "goodness gracious!" (*Explorers on the Moon*, p. 51, 10).

Sensitivity

When Professor Calculus gets offended and loses his temper, it's not only because he falls prey to his own absent-mindedness and his deafness, he also noticeably struggles to overcome his narcissism, which makes him touchy and makes him lose all sense of humour. (*The Castafiore Emerald*, p. 28, 9 and p. 33, 2).

A man with a big heart

But what of these foibles and flaws, when they are compared with Calculus's positive attributes?

The generosity that leads him to offer Marlinspike Hall to Captain Haddock (*Red Rackham's Treasure*, p. 59, 2).

The gratitude that he shows towards Haddock in particular, who he thanks profusely (*Red Rackham's Treasure*, p. 56, 6), going so far as to run and hug him (*Destination Moon*, p. 8, 4), and even to kiss him on the cheek (*The Picaros*, p. 46, 7).

The enthusiasm he shows, for example throughout the lunar mission, and which, much to the dismay of Captain Haddock, causes him to say "we shall return" to the Moon once they had returned to Earth. (*Explorers on the Moon*, p. 62, 7).

His chivalry. The professor appreciates feminine charms, and blushes like a shy teenager when Bianca Castafiore, who he has courted as discretely as he has persistently, kisses him to express her appreciation for the roses that he created for her (*The Castafiore Emerald*, p. 56, 9). He also knows just what to say when paying Peggy, the wife of General Alcazar, who appears wearing hair rollers, the compliment of kissing her hand (*Tintin and the Picaros*, p. 41, 7 and 8).

Calculus: a father figure, or a big baby?

Clad as he is in what psychoanalysis would term to be paternal trappings – the hat, the false collar, the goatee, the raincoat and the umbrella – Calculus can be considered to be a father figure.[18]

However, his reactions to things are sometimes reminiscent of those of a child.[19] For example, the way he trembles in his nightgown when afraid is altogether childlike. (*The Seven Crystal Balls*, p. 33, 12).

On several occasions, he indulges in childishness that takes a dangerous turn and worries Tintin and Haddock.

For example, when he blows up part of Marlinspike Hall (*The Land of Black Gold*, p. 62), or when he leaves Marlinspike without warning Haddock, who only finds out once he is leaving – and we know what the dramatic consequences of him running off like that are. (*The Calculus Affair*, p. 12, 9).

Look out! . . . He's there! . . . He's after me! . . . He's coming! . . .

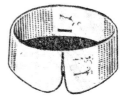

A selection of the false collars worn by Calculus.

18. "At the same time as he discovers an ancestor, all the more admired because he is distant and imaginary, Haddock meets another father, nearby and ordinary, in the person of Calculus." (Jean-Marie Apostolidès, Les métamorphoses de Tintin, Seghers, 1984, p. 158).
19. Serge Tisseron considers Calculus to be "ultimately the figure of Hergé, who represents the best of a gentle and obedient child, preferring to suddenly become deaf, rather than to believe that someone is lying to him or that someone is hiding something from him." (Serge Tisseron, Tintin et le secret d'Hergé, the Hors Collection edition, 1993, p. 77).

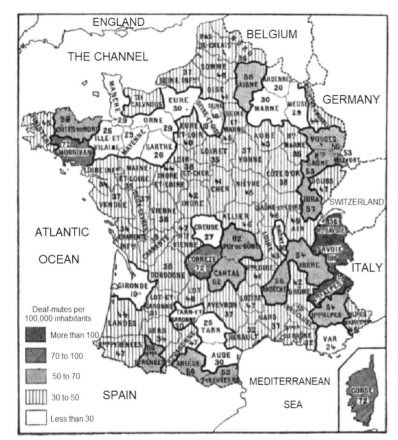

Distribution of deaf-mute people in France. *Larousse médical*, 1903.

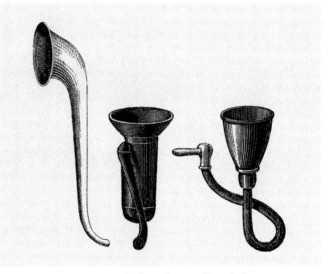

Ear trumpets similar to those used by Calculus.

Tormented by the constant turmoil of an enormous intellect, Professors Sarcophagus and Philippulus – both troubling examples of mad scientists – end up losing their minds.

Equally eccentric, Calculus displays a focus so complete on his interior world that it culminates in his inability to effectually hear the external world.

DEAFNESS AND THE HEARING IMPAIRED

Although, like madness, characters' deafness contributes to disrupting meaning within The Adventures of Tintin, it nonetheless does not prevent communication with other characters.

As Frédéric Soumois wisely observes, "all communication is therefore distorted, not stopped or delayed, and not prevented. This deafness protects the scientist's positive attributes but causes constant short circuits in his relationships with others, who understand him, but can't make him understand them. If he were completely deaf, then the inability to understand others would further contribute to misunderstandings.

However, Calculus is not completely deaf; he is merely "a little hard of hearing".[20]

While allowing the adventure to continue thanks to his inventions, Calculus sustains the comedy already created by the Thompsons, and which is largely based on constant mishearings.

20. Frédéric Soumois, Dossier Tintin Jacques Antoine 1987, p. 187.

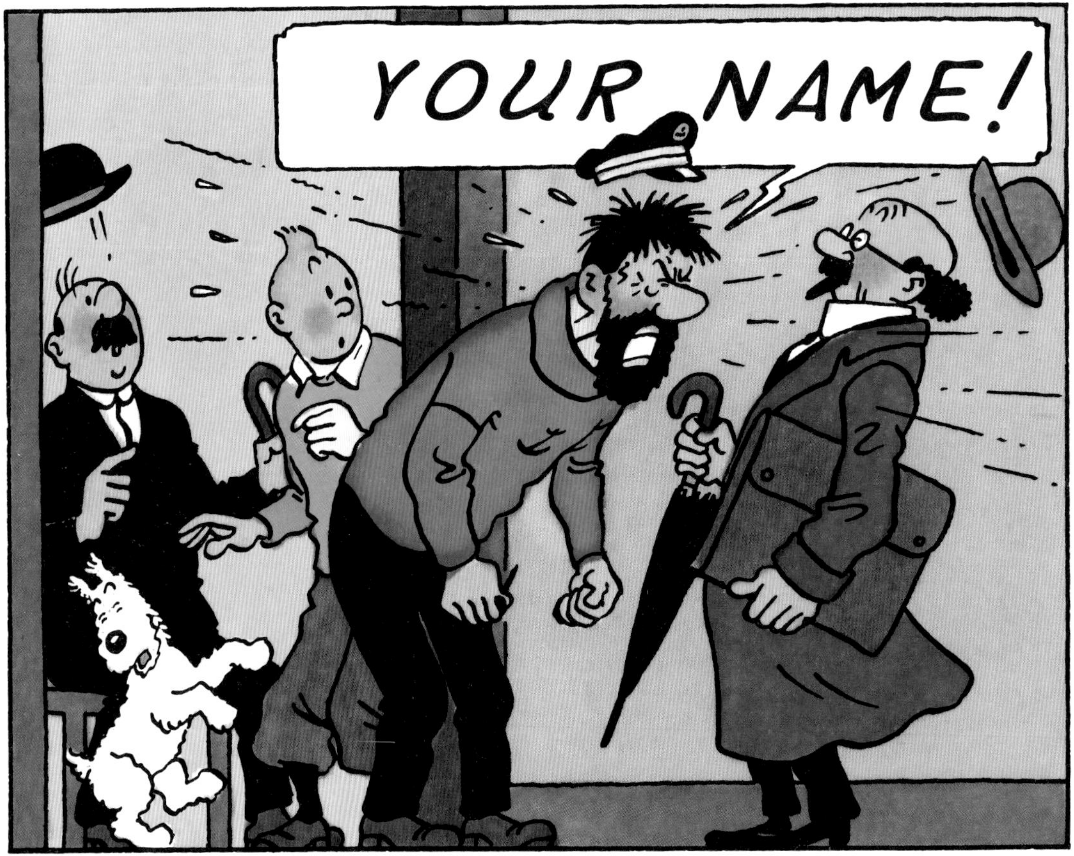
YOUR NAME!

Tervuren, Belgium, 29 November 1967.

Dear Sir,

As a subscriber to the Tintin magazines, I have followed several of Tintin and Snowy's adventures with interest. Each new story was followed eagerly, as much by my married brothers as by me.

Regrettably, I noticed that since "Destination Moon" and in general more and more, the Tintin stories make a joke of mocking people who suffer from a distressing disability: deafness.

These references made through the character of Mr Calculus (examples can be found in the final two pages of "Flight 714 for Sydney"), disguised as a mixture of absent-mindedness and deafness, recall only too well the sad experiences lived by deaf people and only serves to encourage those laughing to make fun of them.

Some time ago, the journal of the Belgian League against deafness picked up on this, and, referring to your previous books, alluded to this, specifically with this sentence: "If Mr. Calculus were blind, why make fun of deaf people? it." If we respect the blind, why make fun of deaf people? Their disability is as distressing as that of blind people, and their lives are also full of problems and difficulties, the extent of which can only be guessed by those who have frequent contact with them. They are already made too much of a target in many gags. This handful of smiles does not outweigh the suffering this creates.

Being myself among those who cannot hear so well, I object to such allusions, which only serve to rub salt on an already open wound.

I am not asking you to revise what has already been published, as it is unfortunately too late. It would, however, be a shame if, in future, stories of such merit as those of Tintin and Snowy continued to contain similar references, which contravene every method for educating young people.

This is why I am appealing to your understanding, with the aim of avoiding these illusions to those – who are more numerous than one might imagine – which seem innocuous, but which revive an underlying suffering.

Certain of soon being able to read about Tintin and Snowy's latest adventures and fully enjoy them, I offer you my best wishes.

Brigitte Bennert

Brigitte BENNERT,
"Les Vallons"
Moorsel – TER-

Miss Brigitte BENNERT
"Les Vallons"
Moorsel – TERVUREN

Dear Miss Bennert,

Of course, regarding content, you're quite right: one should not make jokes concerning deaf people. Neither should one make people laugh at the expense of people who stutter, people who are overweight, English people with big teeth, pig-headed Germans, clumsy people who stumble over every rug they come across, people who butcher the foreign language in which they are valiantly attempting to communicate, etc, etc... An author should not give in to these temptations. Why might he give in in this case, all the same? Because if he were to respect the principles of kindness, writing satirical fiction would become impossible.

As you can see, I am not pleading innocence. But in the case of Calculus, I would like to cite mitigating circumstances. The professor is not a pitiful invalid: he is not the equivalent of a blind person, rather of someone who is short-sighted; his half-deafness is due to age and obviously not congenital; his difficulties do not result from him being in any way "inferior," rather they come from a surfeit of self-confidence on his part. Psychologically, he is not disadvantaged by his hearing impairment, which did not prevent him becoming a brilliant scientist and a man who elicits ridicule far less than he does respect and affection.

I have never made a target of a disabled person such as those you speak of in such moving and compelling terms in your letter: It goes without saying that I will never fall into the trap of doing something so hateful.

I thank you for having written to me so candidly.

Sincerely yours,

Hergé

A source of misunderstanding

Calculus's partial deafness is responsible for a huge number of misunderstandings.

Here let us once again hear what Frédéric Soumois, who has neatly analysed the mechanics of these misunderstandings, has to say: "In effect, his hearing picks up next to nothing, except the sound at the ends of phrases. Convinced that he can hear well, he imagines a new sentence with similar sounds but with a different meaning, which he attributes to his interlocutor, and on the basis of which he continues the conversation and formulates his response.

This shows Calculus's conversation partner that he has not understood them. The interlocutor then repeats their first remark, somewhat insistently.

Taking this to be a continuation of the conversation, the professor responds unfazed to what they say, with a remark as incongruous as his first response. This pattern can be repeated indefinitely."[21]

Calculus makes virtually no appearances that are free of these misunderstandings.

21. Frédéric Soumis, Dossier Tintin.

What progress there has been since the days of Professor Calculus's ear trumpet!

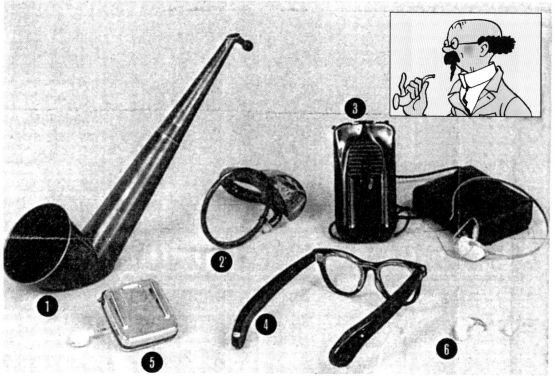

A LONG HISTORY. 1. An early 19th century metal ear trumpet. It resembles Professor Calculus's. 2. A tortoiseshell trumpet with headpiece of the same era. 3. A 1920s device with a lamp unit. 4. Listening glasses, from 1957. 5. Transistor unit, from 1954. 6. Programmable earloop, from 1992.

Understanding auditory signs and signals that are much more basic than spoken language is completely impossible with Calculus's partial deafness. In this way, noises that would alarm anyone else do not bother the professor at all. The ringing of an alarm does not disrupt his sleep (*Destination Moon*, p. 11, 4 and 5), nor does the explosion of a shell in his own bedroom! (*Destination Moon*, p. 17, 19).

In *The Calculus Affair* (p. 7, 6 and 7), he blames moths for the holes that have just been shot in his hat, as he didn't hear the bullets whistle past him. The one occasion on which he thinks he can hear an alarm siren is actually Captain Haddock

Who is it? Did someone knock?

imitating Castafiore's singing (*Destination Moon*, p. 29, 3). Aside from their comic effect, some misunderstandings have a direct effect on the action, because they cause situations that change the course of the adventure.

In *The Seven Crystal Balls* (p. 39, 3 and 4), Calculus is in the garden, where he is kidnapped, because he misunderstood what Tintin said.

In *Destination Moon* (p. 10, 2 and 3), Calculus mishears the Captain's vehement refusal to board the lunar rocket as him agreeing to take part in the expedition, and Calculus's gratitude leaves Haddock speechless, meaning neither he nor Tintin can get out of it.

In *The Calculus Affair* (p. 62, 2 and 8), mistaking the phrase jack-in-the-box for the phrase chicken pox results in Jolyon Wagg's hasty (and welcome) departure from Marlinspike Hall.

In *The Castafiore Emerald* (p. 23, 1 to 11), the professor is questioned about the possible marriage of Captain Haddock and Castafiore by journalists from *Paris-Flash*. Convinced they are asking him about his rose, he involuntarily feeds the rumour.

In *Tintin and the Picaros* (p. 6, 12), by contradicting what Haddock is saying, Calculus validates the charges brought against him by General Tapioca.

Calculus, Bell, Tsiolkovsky and Edison

The fact that the famously hard-of-hearing Cuthbert Calculus devised an ultrasound weapon might seem comical to those who are amused by paradoxes.

Alexander Graham Bell (1847-1922), ended up inventing the telephone in 1876 while making an artificial ear intended for his deaf and mute pupils.

Considered the father of astronautics long before the work of Goddard and Korolev, the Russian professor Konstantin Tsiolkovsky (1857-1935), had a balding head, a moustache and goatee, wore round glasses and suffered from deafness. He developed a prototype rocket and invented motorised roller skates!

As for Thomas Edison (1847-1931), who was hard of hearing, we owe the invention of the gramophone and the telephone headset to him!

Edison

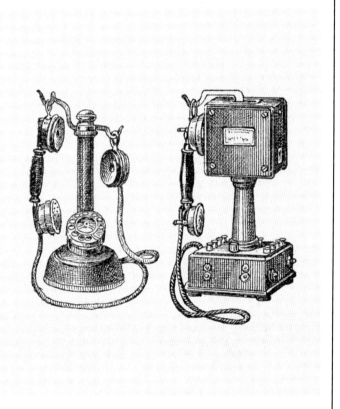

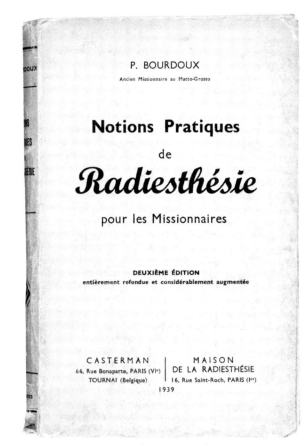

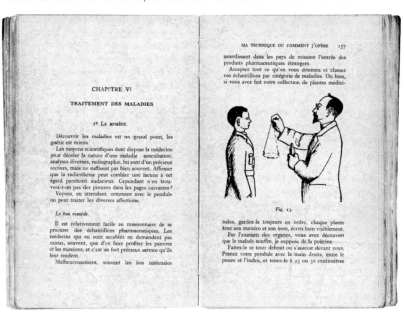

Illustration taken from the book by Père Bourdoux. This could be a tribute to Calculus.

The title page reads: FR. Bourdoux, Former Missionary to Matto-Grosso Practical Concepts of Divining for Missionaries Second Edition, entirely revised and considerably expanded.

The heading reads:
Chapter VI: Treatment of Illnesses

Calculus is made all the more unusual as a scientist in that he does not hesitate to employ radiesthesia, which arouses incredulity, even hostility, from the scientific community.

Nevertheless, don't all good dictionaries remind us that the secondary meaning of the word inventor (from the Latin *invenire*, "to find") refers to someone who finds lost items, treasure, or an archaeological site?

RADIESTHESIA

Calculus's interest in radiesthesia (also called divining or dowsing) coincides with him meeting Tintin and Haddock (*Red Rackham's Treasure*, p. 39, 1). When The Unicorn's search starts to falter, the professor ventures to share the directions given by his pendulum: "Westwards. It's still westwards."

Finally, as if Tintin's purely rational deductions were confirmed by the

non-rational prompts from the pendulum, Calculus in turn follows it into the hall's crypt, where the treasure to be "invented" is hidden.

In *The Seven Crystal Balls*, Calculus's fascination with divining is undiminished. From the very beginning of this adventure, which occurs in an atmosphere of unsettling unreality, the professor appears engrossed in the search for a Saxon burial ground (*The Seven Crystal Balls*, p. 3, 6).

Furthermore, Calculus disappears because he finds an Incan bracelet, when he thought he was going to meet his colleague, Tarragon (*The Seven Crystal Balls*, p. 39 and 40).

During the lunar adventure and *The Calculus Affair*, Calculus is caught up in his scientific inventions, so completely abandons his divining altogether. However, as soon as mystery rears its head, the pendulum reappears! In *Tintin in Tibet*, it is hanging out of the professor's pocket (*Tintin in Tibet*, p. 2, 7). In *The Castafiore Emerald*, it points "in the direction of the gipsy camp." Lastly, on the island of Pulau-pulau Bompa it oscillates several times, although Calculus cannot explain why. (*Flight 714 to Sydney*, p. 28, 6, 7, 8; p. 44, 10, 11, 12, 13; p. 55, 2).

A brief history

In 1929, Father Bouly created the French and International Association of Friends of Dowsing. Several scientists belonged to this, for example Édouard Branly – a member of the Institut Français, Deslandres and d'Arsonval – members of the French Academy of Sciences, the Doctor Meillère – former president of the French Academy of Medicine, and Professor Calculus. The term "radiesthesia" was thus made public. This term, which conjures up images of experiments carried out with the help of pendulums and rods, combines two etymological root words: *radius* from Latin, meaning rod, and *aisthesis* from Greek, meaning perception. According to the French dictionary *Le Petit Robert*, radiesthesia is the "particular sensitivity to the radiation emitted by different bodies" and also the "process of detection based on this sensitivity."

Professor Yves Rocard, former director of the physics department at the École normale supérieure Grande Ecole in Paris, has written several works on the subject of radiesthesia and prefers to refer to it as "biomagnetism."

The magnetism is supposedly explained by the presence of crystals of the natural magnet magnetite (iron oxide) in the human body, which are arranged symmetrically on the attachments of some of our muscles – the arch of the eyebrows, crook of the elbows, knees and heels. So, a magnetiser like Calculus would have more particles of magnetite in his body than people do on average. Professor Rocard would therefore see magnetism as an innate ability that would have developed in prehistoric times.

The theory goes that lightning storms would have magnetised some people. They would have somehow passed this power onto their descendants, most of whom would unfortunately have lost it during the Iron Age. Which suggests:

1. That the lightning that barely misses Calculus when he visits Hercules Tarragon must have re-magnetised

him. (*The Seven Crystal Balls*, p. 30 and 31.)

2. That, in contrast, the Thompson twins, who try in vain to find Tintin, Haddock and Calculus using a pendulum, are completely demagnetised. (*Prisoners of the Sun*, p. 51, 15; p. 53, 5; p. 55, 5; p. 57, 12; p. 59, 15; p. 61, 15.)

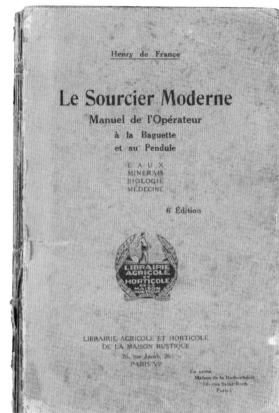

LE SOURCIER MODERNE

...sur la galène, ce qui vous le fera
...t de la main droite. Dans la main
...avez, bien que cela ne soit pas indis-
...autre morceau de minerai. Explorez
...ce le bras gauche étendu. Si le pen-
...vous aurez une première direction de
...recoupez-la en opérant d'un autre point
...aliserez votre gisement souvent à grande
...es mines de houille notamment se décè-
...rt loin.

...croissez votre portée de prospection en
...u-dessus des yeux votre main qui tient le
...et en avant, au préalable, laissé celui-ci
...un bon moment après son réglage.
...la prospection à longue distance n'oubliez
...érifier si après avoir avancé de quelques
...ns ne vous butez pas dans les lignes d'un
...d'eau.

...meilleur procédé de prospection à distance
...ule avec un aimant (ou une boussole blo-
... Vous le posez sur une planchette et fixez
...ier l'aimant dans le plan horizontal en fai-
...tourner un pendule devant le témoin. Quand
...ndule oscille, notez la direction qui est celle
... gisement comme précédemment.
...ous approchez: employez la méthode du plan
...aire en relevant l'angle latéral ou les angles
...éraux, ce qui précisera encore la localisation
...serait intéressant de mesurer ces angles à l'aide
...un grand rapporteur : ces mesures pourraient
...re utiles pour déterminer la nature du minerai.
...Employez également la méthode du méridien.

Pl. III. — La prospection au pendule
Recherche à distance d'un courant ou d'un filon

The title reads: The Modern Dowser: Operator's Manual for the Rod and Pendulum.

Pendulum prospecting

Pendulum

Until the end of the 18th century dowsers were still working with rods and had not yet started to use the pendulum.

However, in 1730, the English physicist Gray noticed that some materials hung from a tensioned wire were attracted by electrified weights.

A short time later, the German scientist Ritter carried out an analysis of the reactions of a pendulum according to the nature of the nearby body (water or metal). From then on, the pendulum became the standard tool for diviners.

Father Bouly (1865-1958) and Father Mermet (1866-1937) were the two pioneers of pendulum radiesthesia.

The research of the former was done on the basis of maps, photographic plans or documents. This is the method Calculus attempted to use to find Red Rackham's treasure.

Father Mermet, in addition to the sources, or groundwater, that he found, uncovered some Saxon burial-grounds and introduced the professor to his technique (*The Seven Crystal Balls*, p. 3, 6).

Baron Beausoleil, Calculus's ancestor

A mineralogist from Brabant and Director of Mines in Tyrol and Trentino, the Baron Beausoleil prospected successfully several times with his wife Martine de Bertereau, in Germany and in Italy. Following this, he returned to France in 1626 at the request of the overseer of the mines of the kingdom, to prospect in the French provinces.

Bankrupted by their searches, the couple approached Cardinal Richelieu in an effort to secure grants, who immediately imprisoned them for witchcraft!

The baron's son felt he had to change the family name to escape the shame that would inevitably reflect on all their descendants; however, he also took great care to choose a name which reflected their scientific interests, for which they had become well-known. In this way, the Beausoleils became the Calculuses.

Professor Calculu[s]

Professor Calculus,
King of scientists and inven[tors]

...ignominious, the reason wh[y]

*Besides an int[...]
bric-a-brac [...]*

TRINGS
& things

ny of my young friends have been
to me once again, to ask me for further
ions of the famous telephone. It is no
ossible for me to expand further on this

I am re[...]
teleph[...]
them[...]

As [...]
assu[...]
the [...]
has [...]

m[...]
w[...]

Real-life Professor Calculus in a hot air balloon

In September, the psychiatrist Bertrand Piccard
from Neuchatel defeated his rivals in the crossing
the Atlantic Ocean in a free balloon. On this great
occasion, we should not fail to notice that he is
the grandson of August Piccard (1884-1962), the
inspiration for Professor Calculus. The physical
resemblance of the
two is clear for the eye to see. This photo of the
Swiss Professor wearing a woven basket lined with
a cushion with strings as a landing helmet was
taken in 1931. It is taken from *Above the clouds*
(*Au-dessus des nuages*), published by Grasset
in 1933. In this book, August Piccard recounted
his two latest ascensions into the stratosphere,
in other words to some 16,000 metres above sea
level. These adventure-filled, "Calculus-esque"
narratives probably inspired Hergé. Let's take the
first flight, in 1931. This started with breaking
a thermometer, the mercury from which mixed
with what was meant to be their drinking [...]
Later, the rope became tangled wi[...]
and became Piccard an[...]
see them full[...]
the S[...]

that we lacked a piece of equipment
in order. I responded that we
in view of all the equip[...]
as much to take [...]
landing [...]
w[...]

France-Soir

5-year suspended sen[tence]
Versailles prison for
"Professor Calculus"

The Goncourt Brothers admired fictional creatures "who have a place in the collective memory just as beings created by God do,

and as if they had a real life on Earth." What would they have thought of Professor Calculus, who sent himself as far as the Moon?

THE UNIVERSALITY OF CALCULUS

Although it's true that his pioneering voyage to the moon contributed to his renown, it must not be forgotten that Calculus's character already included moral and psychological features that would have made the professor a popular model even before the rocket took off. Naïve and very learned, impulsive and sentimental, clumsy yet a

Farewell, Earth!

genius, the professor is now identified with one passion in "the collective memory": inventing.

In spite of dictionaries that do not mention his name and despite historians' heinous silence, Calculus enjoys a glory that even the most brilliant Nobel prize would not have been able to bestow upon him – recognition through language.

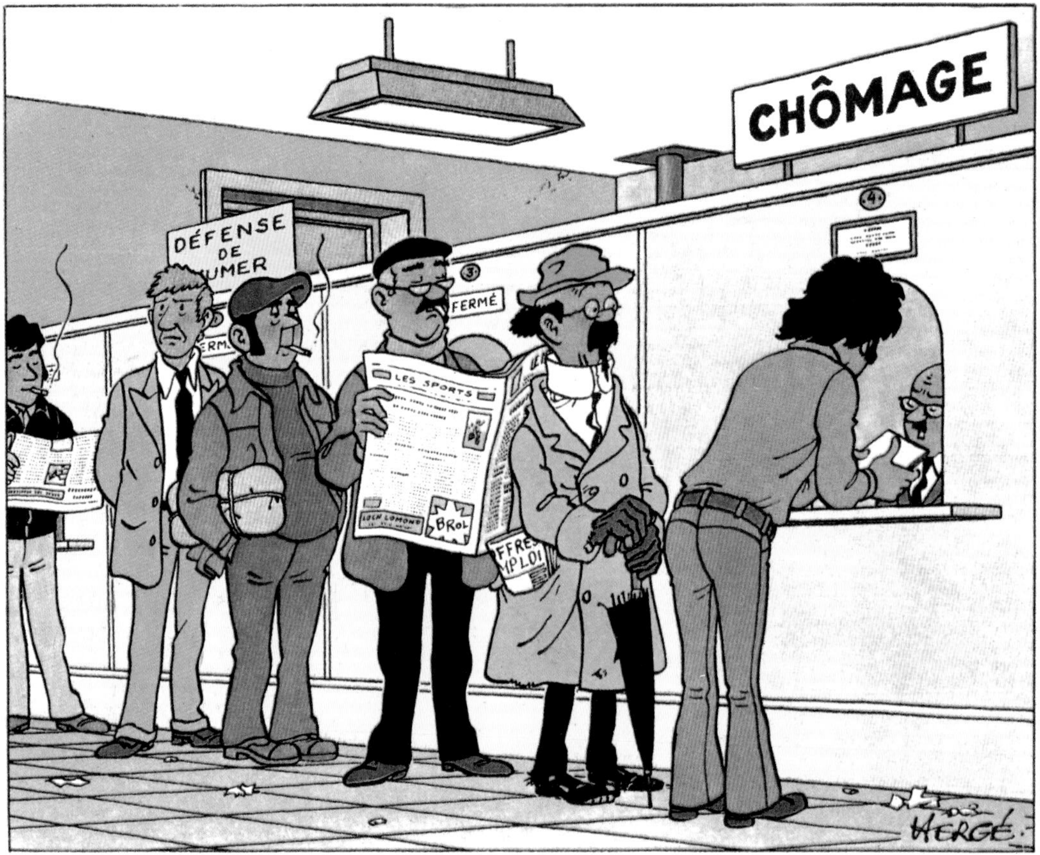

CHÔMAGE
DÉFENSE DE
UMER
FERMÉ
LES SPORTS
BROL
LOCH LOMOND
FFRE
IPLOI
HERGÉ

Professor Calculus is looking for a job! Illustration by Hergé for the business magazine *L'Expansion no. 66.*

From the same author

TINTINOLÂTRIE
Casterman, 1987

BLISTERING BARNACLES
Farshore, 2021

The author wishes to express his great appreciation to *Dominique Cerbelaud*, to *Captain Antoine Champeaux*, an archivist of unmatched ability, to *Philippe Goddin* of the Hergé Foundation, who placed valuable documents at his disposal, to *Philippe Guigon* who left without leaving an address, to *François L'Yvonnet*, the epistemologist, and finally to *Benoît Peeters* for his friendly and wise advice.

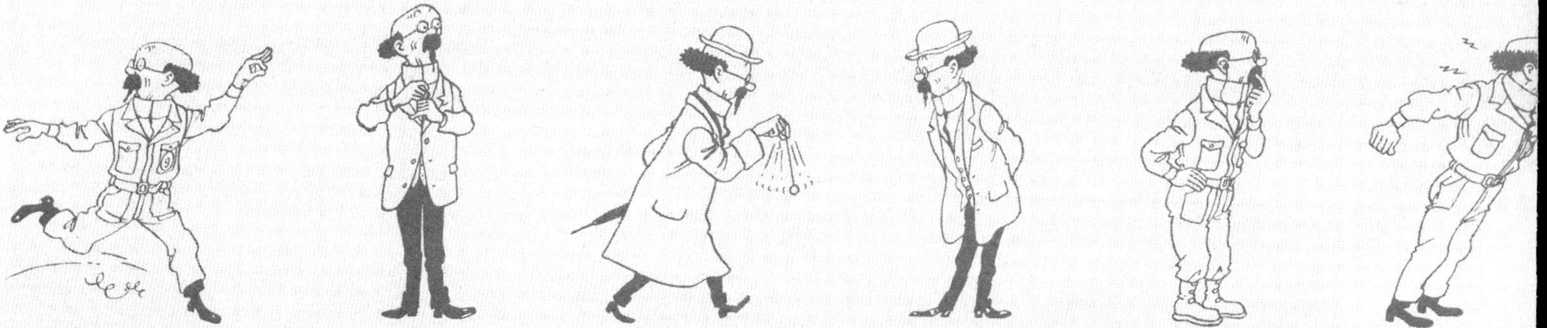
Hergé